Did miracles

"Where are you from?" Jacki asked. It wouldn't have surprised her if he had said a thunderbolt had brought him to her feet. He seemed to have materialized out of nowhere. She could have sworn there hadn't been a soul in the little chapel a moment ago. Yet here he was.

"From up North." She waited for him to elaborate, but he didn't. Instead, he said, "I'm looking for work in exchange for food and lodgings. You wouldn't happen to know of anyone who needs a hand, would you?"

Jacki stared at the tall, rangy man, joy and confusion running riot through her. She had no idea miracles ran so tall.

He was a godsend, pure and simple.

Jacki glanced over her shoulder toward the front of the chapel. "If I had known You worked this fast, I'd have been here sooner."

Dear Reader,

In September, we've got an extra special surprise for you! There's been so much enthusiasm for our DIAMOND JUBILEE titles, that this month we've got two DIAMOND JUBILEE books for you by two of your favorite authors: Annette Broadrick with *Married?!* and Dixie Browning with *The Homing Instinct.*

The DIAMOND JUBILEE—Silhouette Romance's tenth anniversary celebration—is our way of saying thanks to you, our readers. To symbolize the timelessness of love, as well as the modern gift of the tenth anniversary, we're presenting readers with a DIAMOND JUBILEE Silhouette Romance each month, penned by one of your favorite Silhouette Romance authors. In the coming months, writers such as Stella Bagwell, Lucy Gordon and Phyllis Halldorson are writing DIAMOND JUBILEE titles especially for you.

And that's not all! There are six books a month from Silhouette Romance—stories by wonderful writers who time and time again bring home the magic of love. During our anniversary year, each book is special and written with romance in mind. September brings you *Romeo in the Rain* by Kasey Michaels—a sequel to her heart-warming *His Chariot Awaits.* And in the coming months works by such loved writers as Diana Palmer, Brittany Young and Victoria Glenn are sure to put a smile on your lips.

During our tenth anniversary, the spirit of celebration is with us year-round. And that's all due to you, our readers. With the support you've given us, you can look forward to many more years of heartwarming, poignant love stories.

I hope you'll enjoy this book and all of the stories to come. Come home to romance—Silhouette Romance—for always!

Sincerely,

Tara Hughes Gavin
Senior Editor

MARIE FERRARELLA

Her Special Angel

Silhouette Romance

Published by Silhouette Books New York

America's Publisher of Contemporary Romance

To Tara Hughes Gavin,
with endless gratitude

SILHOUETTE BOOKS
300 E. 42nd St., New York, N.Y. 10017

ISBN: 0-373-08744-6

First Silhouette Books printing September 1990

Printed in the U.S.A.

MARIE FERRARELLA

was born in Europe, raised in New York City and now lives in Southern California. She describes herself as the tired mother of two overenergetic children and the contented wife of one wonderful man. She is thrilled to be following her dream of writing full-time.

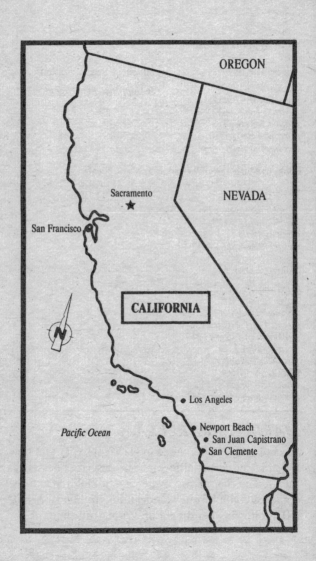

Chapter One

A miracle. What Jaclyn Brannigan desperately needed was a miracle.

Not just a little helping hand, but an honest-to-goodness, genuine, bona fide miracle. Nothing short of that would get her out of the fix she was in. And she was old enough and wise enough to know that the world was fresh out of miracles.

Old enough and wise enough, perhaps, but still a part of Jacki, albeit a small one, believed, clung to the hope that somehow, someway, somewhere a miracle could happen, if only she did the right thing, said the right words. It was a hope built on the faith of the child she had once been. She could see no other option. Jacki did the only thing she could.

She went to the little Serra Chapel in the mission and prayed.

She hadn't been to the mission at San Juan Capistrano for two—no—closer to three years, she thought as she made her way along the worn path around the quadrangle, whose uneven sides had once been measured off by the feet of the Jesuit priests who had originally built it. As a child she had been brought here often by her grandfather. She and her twin Caleb. But Caleb hadn't liked coming to the mission, or going to the ranch, either, for that matter. He saw them both as old, belonging to something in the past. Caleb had always been concerned with the future even then. The future and progress.

But Jacki had loved to walk along the perimeter of the carefully tended rose gardens. She had enjoyed playing hide-and-seek with her grandfather in the narrow passageways, with their musty smell of the long ago and far away. Each corner of the mission had been alive for her with ghosts of the past. She had almost been able to see the Jesuit priests and Indians who had once lived and worked here.

Coming here had always somehow made her feel safe. The mission gave her a link to the past and made her feel a part of it, a part of the thread of life. The mission, along with her grandfather and the ranch, were her anchors, her rocks to cling to in unsteady times.

She needed those anchors today. Needed to feel safe again, to feel that things would somehow work out, even though she could see no logical way that they could.

Jacki slipped into the cool, dark chapel. As if out of respect, the late-afternoon sun remained outside. Only small shafts of light, struggling through the narrow, barred windows on either side of the not quite fifteen-foot-wide chapel, offered any illumination apart from the eternal light that hung from the roof, a beacon to the troubled who came seeking help.

Well, she certainly needed help, Jacki thought, needed it more desperately now than when her parents had died in that plane accident eleven years ago. Then there had been somewhere to turn. Her grandfather had come through for her, taking in both her brother and herself. He had given them a home, never asking for anything in return.

Now he needed her, and she hadn't a prayer of coming through for him.

Prayer.

Jacki smiled ruefully, suddenly remembering what had brought her here in the first place. She moved through the silent, empty chapel and knelt in a wooden pew near the front. The narrow, unpadded kneeler felt hard against her knees, as hard as the world that existed just beyond the chapel's doors.

A sigh escaped Jacki's lips as she brought her hands together before her.

Things were going to be all right, she told herself, her hands clasped in supplication, even as the words formed in her mind.

A small, self-deprecating smile curved the corners of her mouth. To believe that would mean she would have to defy all logic, to shut her eyes to the stark, black-and-white lines of reality. She'd have to forget about the Past Due notices she had been juggling, the date for the final second trust deed payment that was coming closer and closer. She'd have to think with her heart instead of her head.

Thinking with one's heart didn't impress bankers, and she needed not only to impress the bankers, but pay them. And therein lay the problem. There was nothing to pay them with. Nothing—except for the old ranch, her grandfather's precious ranch.

Unless, of course, the miracle materialized.

She closed her eyes and leaned her forehead against her clasped hands. It was November, a little more than a month before Christmas. Christmas was the time for miracles, wasn't it? she demanded silently in despair. Wasn't there one lying around somewhere, one small miracle to spare?

"Not for me," she whispered softly, anguish and frustration in her voice. "For him. For Grandpa. He doesn't deserve to be turned out of his ranch, not after fifty years."

Her voice echoed back to her.

Jacki swallowed, pushing down the growing lump in her throat. Her thoughts were beginning to ramble incoherently, but she was at her wit's end, afraid that the ranch would be lost.

And it was partially her fault, hers and her brother's.

Caleb could help them, she thought bitterly. But practical, business-oriented, successful Caleb, with his growing Newport Beach practice and his country-club, lawyer friends wouldn't help. He had stated the fact very simply, very coolly. She had swallowed her pride and all but begged him. Begging didn't suit her well. She might as well have saved her breath and her pride for all the good it had done her. He had expounded on how sensible it would be for her to let the ranch go.

For her or for him? Jacki had retorted angrily before she stormed out of his office. The ranch belonged to the three of them. Her grandfather had put the deed in all three of their names just after he took them in. And then he had mortgaged the ranch so that he could send both of them to college.

Three lean years and a reversal of business caused by circumstances beyond her grandfather's control had eventually brought them to where they were today. All that—and the bills that had mounted from her grandfather's accident. In an effort to keep the bank from foreclosing, Malcolm Brannigan had kept up the payments and continued to run the ranch by selling off small parcels of land. But he'd stopped abruptly, saying that he'd rather cut off his own hand than cut up any more of his land. And so now they were at a temporary stalemate with fate. But not for long.

The land on which the horse ranch stood was worth a great deal. What Caleb saw in his share was capital gains profit being kept from him.

Jacki, on the other hand, saw dreams to be realized. Her grandfather's dreams. Dreams that would never come to pass once the bank foreclosed.

Jacki felt lost and alone as she knelt in the quiet chapel. Her mind searched in vain for words. She had forgotten how to pray. All the formal prayers she had been taught as a child were so many sentences strung together. They didn't begin to express the pain in her heart, the desperation in her soul.

She stared fixedly at the red tile floor before the altar. Three hundred years ago, the cherrywood altar with its gold leaf overlay had been loaded onto a ship in Barcelona and sent halfway around the world to come to rest here. Its safe arrival in the New World had been heralded as a miracle.

A miracle. It kept coming back to that. She needed a miracle.

She couldn't idly sit by and watch the bank take the ranch. And yet, unless something happened, something to make the small horse ranch become profitable again, something to stave off the bank until spring, that was what was going to happen.

Jacki felt helpless and hated it. This morning the last hand had ridden away from the ranch, leaving apologies in his wake. She couldn't very well blame Joe. There wasn't any money left with which to pay him, and she couldn't expect the man to work on faith and hope. There was precious little of that to spare, as it was. And in thirty days even it would be gone.

Thirty days. She had thirty days to make the second trust deed balloon payment or face foreclosure. What in heaven's name was she going to do?

"If You have a little miracle lying around to spare, I could certainly use it," she murmured under her breath, directing her words heavenward.

With a sigh she rose. She had to get back. It would be evening soon, and she didn't like leaving her grandfather alone. Besides, she needed to turn in early. Without Joe there, all the chores were hers now. Wheelchair-bound for the past three years, her grandfather had been relegated to the position of adviser. But advice didn't feed horses or mend fences.

For a moment she remained standing in the pew. She gripped the rough edges of the bench in front of her. It was as if she were trying to find something tangible to hang on to. Maybe, she thought, she was hoping for a thought to hit her, an inspiration she could fly with. Something. *Anything.*

Jacki knew she could easily give in and let the bank take the ranch. Mr. Saunders, the bank president, had told her that the money that would be left over after the bank auctioned off the ranch and collected its due would go to her grandfather. The two of them could go away and start fresh somewhere else. There were many things she could do to provide for both of them. But it wouldn't be the same. Not to her grandfather and not to her. She had had that path opened to her before, when she graduated from college, but she had chosen not to take it. She belonged on the ranch, just like her grandfather did. Nothing had happened to change that. If anything, she was more determined than ever to hang on. She just needed help in doing it.

Slowly she moved out of the pew. "No use crying about the past or the future."

Jacki stopped at the small tier of offering lights that burned near the entrance of the chapel. She dug into the pocket of her jeans, pulled out a quarter and deposited it in the small slot beneath the candles. She heard it clink softly as it joined other coins.

"Sorry," she murmured to whatever power might be watching over her. "It's all I have to spare."

She took the long taper that stuck haphazardly out of the small container of sand next to the offering lights. Gently she touched it to a wick that was already lit. The small flame divided and spread.

Raising the thin taper, Jacki moved it to another candle. A burst of light sizzled as she touched the unlit wick.

"Please," Jacki whispered. "Help."

She stared at the light, wishing she could see things in that flame, wishing a solution would materialize before her eyes. Suddenly feeling foolish, she pushed the taper into the sand, extinguishing the light. Tears began to sting her eyes. She brushed them aside with her fingertips and turned away.

She almost jumped when she saw him. She hadn't heard anyone come up behind her. Her heart pounded simultaneously in her ears and chest as she looked up.

He had been watching her for a few minutes. From where he had been standing in the back of the chapel, it had been too difficult to discern her features, but the woman praying in the front pew was troubled. That much Gabriel could tell. It was the set of her shoulders, the soft sigh that echoed within the old adobe walls. Now that he saw her face, it was there in her brown eyes and the set of her jaw. No one so young and pretty should be this unhappy, he thought.

"Sorry, didn't mean to startle you." The voice belonging to the tall, serious-looking stranger was deep, low. Steady. "I wanted to wait until you were finished praying."

"I'm finished." The words formed slowly on her lips. He had the most incredible light blue eyes she had ever seen. They mesmerized her. She had the oddest sensation that they could see right into her mind and read her thoughts. She moved aside as if in a trance. "I didn't mean to block the candles. You can light one now."

"I wasn't waiting to light a candle. Fact of the matter is—" a small smile lifted the corners of his mouth "—I haven't any money to spare. I'm what you call temporarily between jobs." There was no embarrassment in his words, nor any proud defiance, either. Just a simple statement of fact.

"What is it you do?" The question came naturally, even though Jacki realized a moment later that it sounded as if she was prying. One look at the stranger's face told her that he didn't see it that way.

He shrugged casually, the denim jacket moving closely with the outline of his shoulders. Muscles won from hard work rippled. "A little bit of this, a little bit of that. Ranching, mostly."

"Ranching?" she echoed. And he needed a job. Badly. A miracle? The question seemed to flash through her mind. Well, why not? Why not just this once? Jacki realized that she felt the slightest bit giddy. "Where are you from?"

It wouldn't have surprised her if he had said a thunderbolt had brought him to her feet. He seemed to have materialized out of nowhere. She could have sworn that there hadn't been a soul in the little chapel a moment ago. Yet here he was.

"From up north." She waited for him to elaborate, but he didn't. Instead he said, "I'm looking for someone who might be willing to give me some work in exchange for food and lodgings. You wouldn't happen to know of anyone, would you?"

Jacki stared at the tall, rangy man, joy and confusion running riot through her. She had no idea miracles ran so tall. He had a face that had seen more than its share of the hard side of life. Yet the small, fine lines around his mouth and eyes appeared to be smile lines rather than ones that came from frowning. And his high cheekbones gave him a proud, almost regal appearance.

He was a godsend, pure and simple.

Jacki glanced over her shoulder toward the front of the chapel. "If I had known You worked this fast, I'd have been here sooner."

She hadn't meant to say the words aloud. They had slipped out in her unabashed enthusiasm. If she could find a man to help her work the ranch, then maybe, somehow, she could find a way to meet that bank note, as well. But she wasn't going to hang on to a ranch hand, even one who came as cheaply and as mysteriously as this one, if he thought the person he was working for was slightly touched in the head.

She turned back to the tall stranger, fully expecting him to make some sort of comment about her odd behavior.

Instead there was an easy, tolerant smile on his lips. She liked him instantly.

Jacki gave him the warmest smile she had. It rose from her toes and filled her, radiating to every corner. "As a matter of fact I do. This may be your lucky day." It certainly is mine, she thought. "I happen to be looking for someone."

They stepped out of the chapel together. In the courtyard, in the light of day, her momentary thought of divine intervention faded. It was some sort of lucky coincidence, that was all. God had better things to do than ride to her rescue.

"Oh?" The stranger looked at her, an expression of amusement on his face.

Jacki suddenly realized that she had worded her statement badly. "I mean I have a ranch a few miles from here."

He nodded his head, apparently assuming that more was coming. "Sounds good."

Honesty made her continue. "It gets worse." He looked rather quizzical, but didn't prod her for an explanation. Jacki had no way of actually knowing, but something made her think that here was an infinitely patient man. "And I need a ranch hand, but I can only afford to pay you in food and lodging."

"So far I don't see any problem. That's all I asked for."

Looking into his eyes made her lose her train of thought. Shifting beneath the piercing, blue gaze, Jacki nodded, then began to walk through the passageway that led past the rose gardens. "Yes, that's all you asked for. So," she said and turned, facing him suddenly, "what do I call you?" Besides a lifesaver, she added silently.

"Gabriel. Gabriel Goodfellow."

What an unusual name, she thought. And how appropriate. He certainly was a good fellow in her eyes, appearing on the scene when he did. And wasn't the Archangel Gabriel the one who led the fight into the fray, or did she have her archangels confused? "I'm Jaclyn Brannigan."

Gabriel tipped the worn black Stetson with two fingers and looked every inch the cowboy. "Ma'am."

"The ranch isn't big enough anymore for you to call me ma'am. Jacki'll do."

She extended her hand to him. He took it, and she felt the strength in his grip. Strength and something more. What, she wasn't quite sure, but once again she had the feeling that he had been sent to her, and to her alone. She would have thought the heat was getting to her, but it wasn't a warm day. It was rather chilly, even though she didn't feel it anymore.

"So—" She cleared her throat, trying to clear her mind, as well. "How soon can you start?"

He let the small hand slip from his a bit reluctantly. Her hand felt good. Soft, yet sturdy. He'd bet that she did a great deal of the work on the ranch herself.

"How does now sound?"

She thought of the section of fence that Joe had left in disrepair. "It sounds wonderful."

She led the way down the winding path toward the exit from the mission grounds. A flock of pigeons scattered as she walked by, shuffling angrily until they could once more reach the feed thrown to them by amused tourists. Gabriel fell into step next to her. She expected him to say something or at least ask a few questions about the ranch. But he seemed to be content just to walk with her.

What a strange man, she couldn't help thinking.

She passed through the iron gate and onto the street, then waited until he joined her. "Mmm, do you need to go and get anything, notify anyone?" She looked at him as he stood with his hands shoved casually in his back pockets. "Pack a toothbrush?"

"I can send for my things tomorrow, although there isn't anything of value." He paused, as if thinking things through. "Except for my horse."

Even though he looked like a cowboy, the fact that he had a horse, when he didn't seem to have anything else, surprised her. He sounded as if he were straight out of some Western movie. "Your horse?"

"Yes, ma'am—Jacki." He flashed her a smile as he corrected himself. "I left him stabled with some friends while I went looking for work."

That was the longest sentence she had managed to get out of him. Encouraged, she pressed her luck further. "You don't own a car?"

"No."

The light at the corner turned green, and she moved quickly to get across. Her stripped-down Jeep was parked at the curb, halfway down the next block. She couldn't imagine getting around Southern California without some means of transportation at her disposal. "Then how did you get to the mission?"

He grinned at her naiveté. "Hitched."

Yes, she could see him doing that. "Do you live around here?"

"Not really."

"I see."

No, she didn't see. Not by a long shot. Was he a vagrant? Had she in her desperation picked up someone who was an unsavory character? An escaped convict? A who-knew-what? She hurried to reach her Jeep. The feel of the car's door handle was reassuring.

As if he read her mind, Gabriel held up hands that were tanned by the sun and callused by hard work. "I'm a little down on my luck, but you don't have anything to fear from me."

It was his eyes that reassured her, they and his tone of voice. There was something infinitely comforting about the tone. It coaxed trust from a person. With a little practice, if he was of that persuasion, she was certain that he could sell Florida swampland to people as vacation property. At this point she had very little to lose, and if he was down on his luck, well, she knew what that was like. She and her grandfather had been down on theirs ever since Seawater had broken his leg. Having the thoroughbred destroyed had been the hardest thing she'd ever had to do.

Jacki pointed to the battered Jeep. "Get in. It's time I—we," she corrected with a snap of satisfaction running through her, "were getting back to the ranch."

She watched as Gabriel eased his way into the passenger side, his long, lanky frame filling out the space. "I appreciate you taking me on like this."

"I'd hold off on that appreciation until after you see what you have to do to earn a meal."

He laughed softly to himself, and she could almost feel the laughter echo within her. It was a feeling akin to having a sunburst spread its rays throughout her body. His laugh made her feel warm and happy for absolutely no reason at all.

"I've a feeling that things'll work out just fine," he told her.

It sounded suspiciously like a promise. Maybe that was what she was searching for. She didn't want to explore the meaning behind the words. She just wanted to hang on to them and the hope they generated. She could go a long way on a shred of hope. She had done it before.

"Yes," Jacki agreed, running a hand through her dark brown hair. "They probably will, at that."

The funny thing was that for no earthly reason at all she believed it.

With a strange, exhilarating feeling coursing through her body and making her feel supremely optimistic, Jacki started up the Jeep.

Chapter Two

He wasn't saying anything.

Several minutes had gone by since she had uttered her last words, and the man beside her seemed to be perfectly satisfied to sit in silence while they drove to the ranch. She glanced at him as she made a right turn. His body language told her he was completely relaxed, if perhaps slightly removed. It was almost as if he existed on another plane.

Jacki was the one who felt uncomfortable.

No, she thought, reconsidering, *uncomfortable* was the wrong word. He didn't make her feel uncomfortable exactly. The trouble was, she wasn't certain just what he made her feel. "Nervous" was probably the best way to describe her restlessness, but it wasn't the kind of nervousness she experienced while in the company of a stranger she knew nothing about. It was more of an anticipation. She realized that she felt as if she was expecting something to happen.

What, she had no idea.

More than likely, Jacki reasoned, it was all due to the state of mind she was in. In the hushed atmosphere of the chapel, Gabriel's sudden appearance out of nowhere had seemed to be an answer to a prayer. Even now, in the bright sunlight of the late afternoon, with traffic whizzing by in two different directions, she still couldn't quite shake the feeling that somehow this was all part of a dream.

If it wasn't, if she didn't allow herself to believe in it, then she'd be forced to face hard reality. Reality was that the thirty days were going to slip swiftly away, the bank would come, clamp its jaws on the ranch, and that would be that.

Somehow she refused to let herself believe that would really happen. Maybe she needed to deny it in order to keep going.

God, he was a quiet one.

Jacki glanced sideways at Gabriel as they left the tidy shops and buildings of the city of San Juan Capistrano behind them. With his arms folded before his chest and his head tilted forward, her new ranch hand—her only ranch hand—appeared to be dozing.

His clothes were a bit worn, and the heels of his boots were run-down. Not much of a go-getter, she thought. What had he been doing at the chapel? He certainly didn't look like a religious sort of man.

Just what's a religious sort of man supposed to look like, Jak? A man with long, flowing hair, wearing sackcloth and dipped in ashes? she thought, scoffing at herself. She had always criticized Caleb for his tendency to stereotype people, and here she was doing it, too. She was tired, that was all. Tired and frustrated and—

You found someone to work the ranch. Be content with that, she told herself.

She knew she should be satisfied to leave it at that, but couldn't help wondering about Gabriel. What sort of man *was* the guy who dropped out of nowhere and into her life?

His hat was pushed slightly forward to block out the rays of the late-afternoon sun, but not far enough to obscure his profile. He had a strong jaw that blended in well with the fine, chiseled planes and angles of his face. It was an honest face, she decided, a trustworthy face, belonging to someone who happened to need a helping hand.

Don't we all? she added silently as she took a turn and headed southeast.

The worn, black Stetson paled against the black of his long, gleaming hair that curled ever so slightly against the back of his neck. A hundred years ago he might have been taken for a desperado in these parts, Jacki mused. Then she thought of his eyes and changed her mind. Eyes like that didn't belong to desperadoes. They were too kind, too warm. He had eyes the color of the sky on a glorious, spring morning. The color of heaven. You couldn't look into eyes like his and feel despair.

She tried to hold on to that thought and let a grain of hope take root within her.

"Something on your mind?"

His voice, low and soft, startled her. "I, um, thought you were asleep."

"Nope."

"Obviously."

She searched for something to cover her momentary embarrassment. She hadn't meant to let him catch her staring at him. He hadn't turned to look at her. How had he known? she wondered. The man seemed to have eyes where none were visible.

"I was just wondering how much you knew about ranching," she lied.

He straightened slightly, pushing his hat from his eyes with the tip of his thumb as he turned in her direction. The gentle smile on his lips had begun in his eyes. "Enough."

She waited for him to explain how much "enough" was. She waited in vain. She had never met a man who hoarded his words so zealously. "Not very long-winded, are you?"

His eyes skimmed over her face. Twenty-three, he judged. Maybe even younger. She should be in the thick of things, enjoying life, not worrying about a ranch. "You learn a lot by listening."

Not when I'm listening to you, she thought. "And you don't give away a lot," she guessed.

He laughed softly. The laugh rippled into the pit of her belly, causing a strange yearning she had no time to wonder over.

"Something like that."

She studied him for a moment, then turned her attention back to the road. Didn't he have *any* curiosity? "Don't you want to know anything?"

Yes, I have questions, he thought, but it's not my place to ask them—yet. "About what?"

"The ranch," she said in exasperation. "Your job. Whether the foreman will beat you and make you work from sunrise to sundown."

"You don't have a foreman."

She swung her head around to look at him. The Jeep swerved.

"Hey, steady." He put his hand over hers on top of the steering wheel.

She looked at their joined hands and then back at him. "How did you know that?"

"Know what?" He withdrew his hand. The touch of a woman's hand had felt good. Other than in the handshake that had sealed their bargain, he hadn't touched a woman in a very long time.

She tried to keep her mind on the road. Because there were only a few cars passing by now, she could relax a little. She knew the way back to Los Caballos Royales in her sleep. "That I didn't have a foreman."

"You'd hardly be taking on a man for just room and board if you had money to pay a foreman."

Her pride was wounded. "Well, we did have a foreman."

"What happened to him?"

"He left six months ago." Jacki turned slightly in her seat, challenging him to ask her for more information. He was stronger than she gave him credit for. He didn't follow up her statement with an inquiry. "Don't you want to ask why?"

"Only if you want to tell me."

She shook her head in disbelief. "Well, you're certainly not pushy, I'll give you that."

"Nope." He folded his arms again and leaned back. The Jeep was not built to accommodate his long frame, but Gabriel had learned to make the best of situations a very long time ago.

"How about lazy?" she suggested, wanting to see if anything would get a rise out of him.

Gabriel arched a brow and studied her for a moment, weighing his words. When he finally answered, it was in a mild tone of voice. "I rest on my own time. The way I see things, I don't start working for you until we reach your ranch."

Jacki bit her lower lip. She didn't know what had made her bait him like that. "I'm sorry. I didn't mean to insult you."

"You didn't. I was just clarifying the matter for you."

"The reason I asked was that I was hoping you'd say you were a hard worker."

"The others slacking off?"

She sighed as she shook her head. "There are no others."

She held her breath, awaiting his response. She saw mild interest pass over his face. Finally he was reacting to something. She savored her triumph.

The road was long and winding, with rolling green hills on either side. Sometimes she liked to pretend that the road went on forever. Now, however, she was glad it didn't. She couldn't wait to get back to the ranch. She knew her grandfather would be pleased by this latest development.

"Just how small is your ranch?"

She laughed, pushing aside the strand of honey-brown hair that suddenly danced across her cheek. "Not *that* small." And then she grew more serious as she remembered. "Once it was a showplace. My grandfather called it El Rancho de los Caballos Royales, the ranch of the royal horses. It's his pride and joy. He bred champion thoroughbreds. It was a thriving horse ranch not that long ago."

"And now?"

He watched as she lifted her chin. Sheer determination was written in the small gesture.

"Now he has a granddaughter who's determined not to see the ranch go under."

"So the ranch is in trouble."

How had she allowed that to come out? She hadn't meant to admit anything of the kind, certainly not to someone she knew only by name and nothing more. Jacki squared her shoulders. "No, it's not." She almost shouted the words at him.

"Then why isn't there anyone else working it?" He wasn't trying to goad her. It was meant purely as a rhetorical question. He valued honesty above all else. He had a feeling that, at bottom, so did she.

"Because—" She faltered. Jacki stared at her hands. She was gripping the steering wheel. She loosened her hold. There was no point in putting up a pretense. He'd find out the truth soon enough. "Because the ranch is in trouble."

Down, but not out yet. She wasn't a quitter. He could see it in her manner. He liked that. "People've been in trouble before and gotten out of it."

She knew that her plight shouldn't mean anything to him. The fact that he was thoughtful enough to offer comforting words of hope struck a responsive chord within her. Maybe he wasn't that devoid of curiosity and basic emotions, after all. She allowed a grateful smile to curve her lips. "That's what I keep telling Grandpa."

"And he believes it?"

"He believes in me."

He caught the sigh that seemed to slip out involuntarily with her words. "That could be a burden."

Yes, it could, but she wasn't about to admit that on top of her last slip. Jacki raised her head a fraction of an inch again. "I'm up to it."

Gabriel held up his hands in surrender. He had no intention of giving her an argument on that score. "You've got my vote."

"Thanks, but what I need is your back, your arms and your legs."

"Them, too. I'd throw in my soul, as well, but I'm kind of partial as to who gets that."

She laughed again, taking pleasure in the act. There had been little to laugh about lately. The red ink in the account book and the mounting unpaid bills had taken humor away from her. "I don't plan to work you that much," she promised with a grin.

"We'll see."

This time when the silence between them returned, she didn't feel uneasy about it. As they drove on, Gabriel spoke when he wanted to, which was fine with her. When he did speak, the sound of his voice was like the low, autumn wind, slightly mournful, slightly sweet. He raised more questions in her mind when he talked than when he didn't. He struck her as a man of mystery, and that intrigued her. He didn't deliberately hide anything, but he didn't embellish on his statements, either. For the first time in weeks, Jacki had something else besides the ranch and her grandfather on her mind.

It felt good.

The ranch house appeared in the distance, small and oddly forlorn against the early-evening sky. Before his accident, her grandfather had always meant to add on to the house, but had never gotten around to it. Now there was no opportunity to do so. But it was home and meant the world to her.

"Well, there it is. El Rancho de los Caballos Royales."

As they drew closer, the effects of time and weather on the house became readily apparent. Jacki brought the Jeep to a halt before the front porch.

Gabriel studied the single-story house in silence. "Needs a little work," he observed.

She pulled up the hand brake, then peered at his lean face. "Are you volunteering?" she asked, a touch of mischief in her voice.

"I do whatever needs doing."

"I'll hold you to that."

He unfolded his long, muscular legs and swung them out of the Jeep. Jacki couldn't help watching in fascination. She felt an odd tingle as she looked him over again. Though he had made no move toward her, had said nothing that could even be slightly misconstrued as a pass, the word *masculine* telegraphed itself throughout her nerve endings and made them flutter in an anticipation that was timeless.

There had been no time for any of that, either, she thought suddenly. She had foregone the exhilarating give-and-take of a male to female relationship for the sake of the ranch. Work had taken up all of her time. It had been her choice.

Her grandfather had recently lamented that all the burden seemed to have fallen upon her shoulders. He had talked of selling then, saying she was missing things that women her age all took for granted. Jacki had countered by scoffing at his words, saying that she had all the companionship she wanted and besides, according to all the latest magazine articles, women were waiting longer and longer to begin that all-important, so-called meaningful relationship. After the ranch was on steady ground, *then* she'd think of things like going out.

Her grandfather had merely snorted, but said nothing more—which was rare. She knew he was grateful to her, but didn't quite know how to go about saying it. The words "Thank you" came hard to him.

She turned now to see her grandfather watching the two of them from the porch. He sat there, a robust, wide-boned man, imprisoned in a wheelchair he could not come to terms with. The wind was up, but he refused to throw a blanket over his legs, refused to admit to any more weakness than he was forced to.

He eyed Gabriel, but addressed Jacki. "I was worried about you, Jak. Thought maybe you finally got some sense in that fool head of yours and ran off along with Joe."

"Joe was our last ranch hand," she explained under her breath to Gabriel. Without thinking, she took his arm as she gestured for him to come meet her grandfather. "He's the one who left this morning." She turned to look at the old man in the wheelchair. "I went to the mission, Grandpa."

"Oh? Is that where you found him?" Malcolm Brannigan's shaggy, gray eyebrows lifted and fell as he stared at the tall, denim-clad man standing next to his granddaughter.

"As matter of fact, yes. I lit a candle and asked for a miracle."

"And that's what they're giving out?" the gravelly voice asked.

Jacki wondered if the man at her side would respond with a sarcastic retort. He had the right. She'd had no idea her grandfather was going to say something like that. "Pay no attention to Grandpa. He gets surlier as the day wears on."

"I can make my own excuses, girl."

"How about your own apologies?" she asked fondly as she mounted the front steps.

She cast a nervous eye toward Gabriel and saw that he looked tolerantly amused by her grandfather. Planting one foot on the top step, he leaned forward. That way they were at eye level with each other. She wondered if he had done that on purpose and decided he probably had.

"Malcolm Brannigan, meet Gabriel Goodfellow." Jacki gestured from one man to the other. "Gabriel's going to be working for his room and board," she clarified for her grandfather's sake when he gave her a quizzical look. Their last discussion this afternoon, before she had driven off, had been about the fact that there was no money left with which to hire someone.

"They were a little short on miracles at the mission right now," Gabriel said, referring to Malcolm's assessment of him. "This being the most popular season for folks to ask for them. I'm the best they could do."

He said it so solemnly that Jacki could have sworn Gabriel was serious. It wasn't until her grandfather's lusty laugh rumbled from his barrel chest that Jacki saw the dry wit behind the younger man's words.

Malcolm nodded. "I like a man with a sense of humor." He glanced toward Jacki. "He's going to work out fine, just fine." Malcolm put out his hand. Gabriel took it, shaking it heartily. "How long do you plan on staying?"

"For as long as you'll have me."

If she didn't know any better, she would have said there was a hidden meaning behind his words. She dismissed the notion as the wanderings of an overworked imagination. She was tired, hungry, and a little dazed at having actually found someone willing to work for next to nothing, who wasn't on his last legs.

"Oh, we'll have you, all right," she assured Gabriel as she stood next to her grandfather. "I wouldn't be able to beat the deal you offered."

He merely smiled at her, and she would have given almost anything to know what was going on behind those
blue eyes of his.

Suddenly she heard the sound of loud barking. She
swung around, just as the Border collie came bounding
from behind the ranch house. She knew in an instant he
was heading for Gabriel. She only had a second to suck
in her breath. "Get out of the way!" she warned. "He
doesn't like anyone but—"

The words died in her throat; she stared in absolute,
speechless wonder. The small, dark collie usually bared
his teeth or at the very least barked noisily at a stranger.
Even those who were familiar to him received his nota-
ble disdain. Once he had actually taken a nip out of
Carlos Montoya, a new ranch hand. Carlos hadn't stayed
around to become an old hand.

This fierce combination of fur and fury came to an
uncertain halt at Gabriel's feet. Rather than loud barking, there was a restrained, confused silence as the collie
sniffed the newcomer. And then, to Jacki's complete
amazement, the dog allowed himself to be stroked on the
head.

"You were saying?" Gabriel asked, kneeling down.
The dog licked his face. Gabriel laughed and playfully
rubbed the animal's back.

"Well, I'll be—" Malcolm muttered, chuckling.

"Sweetheart usually hates people," Jacki mumbled in
confusion, staring at the dog. What had come over him?
And just what kind of a power did this Gabriel Goodfellow possess? She had never seen Sweetheart behave this
way. The dog had been given his name because his behavior was the total antithesis of the word. Her grandfather had said he had never run into anything ornerier

than the Border collie. "Except," she added, "for Grandpa and me. He even growls at my brother Caleb."

"I'd growl at Caleb myself," Malcolm snorted.

"You do," Jacki said mechanically, still staring at her unusually docile pet.

Malcolm leaned forward. "Boy's got no soul," he confided to Gabriel.

Gabriel rose to his feet. "That's been known to happen a time or two."

He spoke as if he had an inside knowledge of human nature, she thought, again wondering who he was and where he came from. And why Sweetheart hadn't taken a piece out of him. Not that she'd wanted him to, of course. But it certainly would have been more natural if he had tried. For that matter, her grandfather seemed to have taken to Gabriel much faster than she would have expected him to. He was usually much more standoffish and critical in his initial appraisal. He liked a man to prove himself.

Well, hadn't she taken to Gabriel pretty quickly herself?

Just who *was* this man?

Gabriel noted the expression on her face. "What's the matter?"

She nodded toward the dog. "I can't get over the fact that Sweetheart didn't try to bite you."

"Would you rather he did?"

"No, of course not. It's just that—" she looked at the animal "—it's like you hypnotized him. I've never seen him like this with anyone else but us."

Gabriel shrugged casually. "I have a way with animals."

"That'll come in handy around here," Malcolm told him. "We've got eight horses—five mares, two geldings and a stallion. But there'll be more," he promised with such complete confidence that Jacki's heart ached.

Gripping the wide wheels, Malcolm turned his chair to face the front door.

Gabriel moved behind him. "Would you like me to push you in?"

Malcolm was fiercely independent and didn't take kindly to offers of help, especially from strangers. Jacki braced herself for the barrage of blue words she knew would follow.

"I'd welcome it, boy."

Jacki gave up. Something strange was going on here. Maybe she was still at the chapel and had fallen asleep in the pew. Maybe this was all a dream.

She looked around for Sweetheart. The Border collie was gone. He was right behind Gabriel, following him inside.

Yes, she thought. Something strange was going on here. Something very strange.

She stood for a moment in the dark, then shook her head as she ran her hands up and down her arms. With a sigh she followed the others inside. She wasn't going to solve anything by freezing.

Chapter Three

Jacki closed the front door behind her. "I don't suppose you have any plans for dinner," she said to Gabriel.

She removed her jacket and tossed it haphazardly. It landed on the edge of the love seat in a corner of the room. It was an utterly masculine room of dark wood and leather, with touches of femininity here and there that Jacki had added over the years. The two complemented each other like a man and woman whose bodies were entwined in a lyrical dance.

Gabriel slid off his Stetson and ran the brim through his hands. He appeared to be considering her question. "I wasn't really planning on dinner."

She pushed up the sleeves of her blue pullover and scrutinized him. It was rather an odd response. "Does that mean you're not hungry?"

"No, that means I wasn't planning on it."

Never one to sit quietly by for more than a few moments, Malcolm took control of the conversation with obvious impatience. "Hell, we've still got enough food left to fill another hungry belly." He hit Gabriel's taut abdomen with the back of his hand.

In Jacki's book, Malcolm's tone and gesture suggested total acceptance.

"You're tall, but by the looks of you, you don't eat much. Join us, boy?"

Jacki found it amusing that Malcolm referred to Gabriel as "boy." If ever there was a man least likely to conjure up thoughts of a boy, it was this new hired hand of theirs. He looked as if he had been born shouldering his own responsibilities. There was something about the way he carried himself, proudly, yet without arrogance. He was comfortable with who and what he was.

She wished she had a handle on exactly what that "who" was. Both Sweetheart and her grandfather's reactions to Gabriel were out of character for them and piqued her curiosity even further. Malcolm Brannigan, though at bottom possessing a kind heart, reserved judgment about people until after he had had time to study and digest their behavior. She had never seen him take to anyone else the way he had taken to Gabriel. But then, perhaps worry and loneliness had tempered his usual wariness, Jacki decided.

Well, whoever Gabriel was, he had to be fed. The idea of cooking for someone new pleased her. She didn't bother to explore the reasons. "I've got dinner in the oven. Pot roast to your liking?"

Gabriel gave a small nod in her direction. "Always was."

"He doesn't talk much," Jacki informed her grandfather with a wink as she walked by the two men on her way to the kitchen.

"Nothing wrong with that," Malcolm called out to her. "She's a fine girl," he told Gabriel, turning around again. "Doesn't mind well, but her heart's in the right place. Stubborn, just like her grandmother." He smiled fondly.

"I heard that," Jacki called from the kitchen.

Malcolm leaned forward. "Big ears, too," he whispered.

Gabriel smiled broadly, amused by the old man. "I hadn't noticed."

"You will," Malcolm promised, rolling his eyes. "You will. Well—" he settled back in his chair "—are you from around here or just passing through?" He motioned with a sun-bronzed hand toward a dark brown sofa. The back of it was draped with a multicolored granny-square afghan that had been Jacki's proud contribution to the room's decor eight years ago. "Sit."

Gabriel sat down and crossed his long legs, resting one ankle across the thigh of the other leg. His boots were worn, but well tooled beneath the dust. "I was visiting some friends and decided to stay awhile." Gabriel set his Stetson next to him.

Though he hardly moved his head, his eyes took in everything about the room, about the man sitting in front of him. He could see that Malcolm was not one who allowed himself to slip into resignation about anything. That was probably where she got it from, Gabriel mused.

"These friends of yours ranchers?"

"No."

In the midst of setting the table, Jacki stopped and peered through the large, arched doorway that separated the two rooms. "He doesn't do very much with questions either, Grandpa."

Malcolm rose slightly in his seat as he turned in Jacki's direction. "I was talking to Gabriel here. You just get on with the pot roast."

"Yes, Grandpa."

"That's better." Malcolm gave a smart nod of his head, but his eyes told Gabriel that he wasn't taken in by Jacki's supposed docile compliance. Gabriel had a feeling that she could more than hold her own in a one-on-one confrontation with her grandfather—and that the old man knew it, as well.

Malcolm settled back in his wheelchair once again. "Well, I guess it's lucky for us that they're not ranchers. Lot of work to be done here." He stared down at his legs, which were useless to him now. "I used to be able to ride from sunup to way past sundown, but those days are gone now." The look in his eyes was full of anger at the injustice of it all.

Gabriel empathized with the old man. He knew what it was like to have no control over his own movements. "Things change," he said kindly.

Malcolm cleared his throat and roused himself. "That they do. That they surely do." He cocked his head back and called out, "Dinner ready yet, Jak?"

Jacki placed a small pot roast surrounded by tiny, round potatoes in the center of the kitchen table. A drop of the meat's juice settled on the blue tablecloth next to the platter and spread, reaching the size of a quarter. Jacki swore under her breath. Carefully she moved the plate over an inch.

"I just managed to save it," she told the old man, tossing off the words as she reentered the living room through the adobe archway. "Ten more minutes and we'd be eating charcoal. I thought I told you to watch it for me."

Malcolm tugged at his beard, avoiding her eyes. "I did. It wasn't going anywhere."

"You're hopeless."

"Never that," Malcolm said as Jacki pushed him into the old-fashioned kitchen. Here there was a brick fireplace where she did a great deal of open-hearth cooking. Somehow she preferred that to using the conveniences that were available to her. It gave food a better flavor. At least to her. She moved her grandfather to the place setting that had no chair.

Warmth. There was warmth here, Gabriel thought as he took his place at the small table. A blind man could see it. It brought back memories from his past, memories that had almost faded from his mind. Almost, but not quite.

However long he managed to stay, Gabriel reflected, he was going to like it here.

"C'mon," Jacki urged Gabriel. "You probably want to see where you'll be staying."

The dishes were stacked in the sink. Normally, she would have done them first. She didn't like putting anything off. Chores had a tendency to multiply. She probably could simply motion Gabriel in the right direction to the bunkhouse, but she didn't want to pass up an opportunity to steal a little time alone with him.

To get a better handle on him, she told herself. Then, because she rarely lied, and never to herself, she admitted that she needed to better understand this strange attraction she felt for him. Gabriel had mesmerized her dog and charmed her grandfather within a matter of minutes, just by being quiet and soft-spoken. Just by being, actually. That fascinated her.

And the fact that she was attracted to him on a level she had scarcely felt before fascinated her even more.

"If it wouldn't be putting you out," Gabriel conceded. His smile told her that he welcomed her company.

"Putting her out? Ha." Malcolm dug out his pipe for his one smoke of the evening. "She's hoping if she stays away long enough, I'll do the dishes."

Jacki eyed the pipe critically. She didn't like him smoking. Anything that might take even a day of his life away from her was the enemy. "The thought did cross my mind."

"Well, have it uncross." Malcolm drew on his pipe, making sure that the match had done its job. A curl of smoke ascended from his lips as he puffed it out. He spared them no more of his attention.

Jacki shook her head. The man was incorrigible—and she loved him dearly. She led the way out of the kitchen and through the living room to the front door. "He's quite a character."

Extending his long arm around Jacki, Gabriel pushed opened the unlocked door and let her step out first. "I like him."

The brisk night air felt cold against her cheek and drew her thoughts away from his nearness. "I'm glad." And she was. She had no idea why it should matter to her that this total stranger should like her grandfather, but it did. "He doesn't take all that well to strangers usually."

Gabriel nodded with a grin. "Like your dog."

"Not quite." Jacki laughed. "Grandpa never took a bite out of a person, although he was probably tempted to with Caleb."

"Well—" she gestured to the building in front of them "—it's definitely not much, but the hands called it home—when they were here." She pushed open the door. It creaked its protest at the invasion. Jacki felt around for the light switch. Finding it, she flipped it on. The long room looked forlorn beneath the dim illumination. "You'll have the run of the place now."

Gabriel moved around the long room. There were two rows of empty bunks running along the sides and a table and chair at either end. The layout was obviously meant to house many men. Now it simply accentuated the emptiness. For a moment there was no other sound except for Gabriel's heels, as they came in contact with the wooden floor.

He turned to face her again. The empty space pleased him enormously. "Where I'm from there were a lot of rooms, but never enough space. This'll do just fine."

She crossed the space between them. He was much taller than she, yet there was nothing threatening about his height. Instead, the opposite was true. It was as if he could protect and shelter whatever came into contact with him.

His answer puzzled her. "Just where are you from?"

"Up north."

He had said that before. Getting information from him was like pulling teeth, she thought. Oddly enough, she was enjoying the challenge. "How far north?"

"Far."

He was better at the game than she was, Jacki thought in admiration. "Is there something you're not telling me, Gabriel?"

He turned away then, his attention seemingly taken up by choosing a bunk. "Lots of things. But I suspect that they'll come up in the conversation by and by, if I stay long enough."

If.

The word shimmered in front of her, taking on breadth and depth. *If*. That gave the situation such a temporary feel. Well, nothing was permanent, even if it appeared to be. She knew that. She had once thought the ranch would be theirs forever. Circumstances had changed and dictated that her grandfather be forced into a position of debt after being solvent for so many years.

She couldn't dwell on what might happen in the future. The fact was that Gabriel had seemingly materialized almost out of thin air, and she was grateful that he was going to stay and work for a roof over his head and three square meals a day. The way things were, she certainly couldn't manage to take care of everything by herself.

Jacki realized that he was studying her. He was probably wondering if it was worth staying here, being subjected to her probing. Yes, she wanted to shout at him. Yes.

"I didn't mean to pry. As long as you haven't killed anyone—" She was rambling again, she thought, chagrined.

"I didn't," he said softly.

"—then that's all that matters around here. That, and how hard you can work. With any luck—" a miracle, she added silently "—I'll be able to pay you soon."

It was time to beat a hasty retreat, before she said anything else that might unintentionally send him on his way.

"We can see if I work hard enough to suit you tomorrow." Sensing her discomfort, Gabriel held the door open for her with one hand. She walked onto the front porch.

"Breakfast is at six," she told him.

"Pancakes?"

The simple request made her smile. Maybe she'd learn things about this close-mouthed cowboy yet. "All you can eat."

"I'll be there."

She was still looking at him and smiling as she descended from the porch. Walking and smiling didn't quite work well together this time. The heel of her boot caught on a loose board. Jacki continued on her way, while her heel didn't. She would have tumbled down the stairs to her everlasting embarrassment had Gabriel not grabbed her hand and pulled her up to him.

And against him.

Tiny pinpoints of light exploded all through her body as she looked at him, the gasp at her sudden stumble having just filled her lungs. She tried to let her breath out slowly, but it escaped in a ragged, telltale surge. She was acutely aware that their bodies were touching.

Her eyes on his mouth, her mind on the way he felt against her, she self-consciously mumbled, "Thank you."

"No need for thanks. If you broke your leg, you wouldn't be able to make pancakes." His eyes smiled at her.

"Lucky for me you like pancakes."

His hands fitted well around her waist. They were so large, they almost spanned it completely. And for a moment she thought she felt his hands touching her everywhere, even though he hadn't moved them. Then he did. But it was to let her go.

Why hadn't he kissed her? she wondered with a sudden pang that surprised her by its intensity. The logistics had been right. And she knew she wasn't sending out signals that he could perceive as being negative. Was there someone else? She'd have to find that out before she allowed the sensations she was feeling at this moment to get any greater hold on her.

Dusk had enshrouded the world while they had been inside, eating, and now the stars were coming out. She looked at the sky as she carefully stepped off the porch, holding on this time. It had been a long while since she had seen so many of them. Or perhaps it had merely been a long time since she had paid attention to such simple pleasures.

"It's a beautiful night," Gabriel said, as if reading her mind.

"I don't remember ever seeing the stars look so clear. Most of the time they're not even out at all."

He walked up behind her. "They're always there. They're meant to guide us. Sometimes, though, you just can't see them."

She sensed his nearness rather than heard it. It was as if they occupied the same wavelength for a moment. "You sound like a sailor."

"The stars are there for everyone, not just sailors. Everyone loses their way at one point or another."

She turned to look at Gabriel. What an odd thing to say. Was he just making idle conversation, or did he somehow feel that she had lost her way? Because she had. These days she didn't know which way to turn or what to do. That was what had taken her to the mission this afternoon.

"Does everyone find it?" she asked, her eyes on his. In the dark they looked almost black. But they were still warm, still strangely comforting.

"They do if they look hard enough."

She felt the strongest urge to stand on her toes, take hold of the lapels of his denim jacket and kiss him. She was beginning to entertain the thought that she was losing her hold on reality at a very rapid rate. "Part ranch hand, part philosopher. I think I have myself quite a deal for three square meals a day."

He moved away from her, retracing his steps up the stairs without looking at them. He managed to avoid the loose board, she noted. "That'll be for you to say."

"Yes, it will. Well, good night, Gabriel." She turned away.

"Good night." His voice followed her.

Jacki shoved her hands deep into the pockets of her sheepskin jacket and walked toward the main house. She knew that he was watching her. It made her feel warm. And alive.

The heat inside the house assaulted her cheeks. She felt the color rise and was grateful for the camouflage. She didn't want any knowing looks from her grandfather. The door banged shut behind her. She scarcely heard it.

"Get lost coming back?"

It took her a moment to recollect her thoughts. Her mind had drifted a million miles away, floating to no particular destination. She felt good.

The television set was on, a given after dinner. Her grandfather liked to settle in before the small set and watch until after eleven. He felt it his duty to critically edit the nightly news broadcast.

Jacki took off her jacket and let it settle on the sofa. "We talked a little."

Instead of making a comment about leaving him alone, Malcolm nodded his approval. Maybe, Jacki thought, this was a time for miracles, at least tiny ones.

"Nice fella. Come join me. They're playing my favorite movie." He pointed toward the action on the small set. "*It's a Wonderful Life.*"

Jacki thought of the account books on her desk in the den. It was nearing the end of the month, and she really had to go over them. But they weren't going anywhere, and somehow she didn't feel like spoiling her mood by looking at depressing figures tonight.

With a grin she sat down on the sofa. "Is that an observation?"

"No, that's the movie. Don't you know anything, girl?"

"Only what you tell me, Grandpa." She leaned over and tugged at his beard affectionately.

"Then listen to this. I might complain once in a while—"

"Once in a while?"

He continued as if she hadn't said anything. "But it *is* a wonderful life. Just you wait, Jak. Things turn around if you work hard enough."

She laced her fingers around her knee and leaned back. "So he told me."

"He?"

"Gabriel."

Malcolm nodded sagely, agreeing with the absent man. "Knew he was a smart boy, the minute I laid eyes on him." He motioned with a bowl of potato chips toward his granddaughter. "Found some potato chips. Want any?"

"You can eat after that dinner?"

"Jak, I can *always* eat." To prove it, he munched a handful of chips, then waved his hand at the screen. "Now watch the movie. It might make you feel better."

She wasn't like him. She couldn't let her mind wander in a fantasyland created in Hollywood. It didn't help her forget about the wolf—or the banker—at their door.

"The only thing that'll make me feel better is if the bank lost the note on our second trust deed—or if Mr. Saunders suddenly had a heart transplant and learned what to do with it."

She really ought to get at those books, she thought again. And the dishes were still waiting. Then she looked at Malcolm's face. She sat in silence for a moment, debating with herself. Well, the very least she could do for her grandfather was join him in this, one of his few pleasures.

She ran her hand along the crocheted doilies that her grandmother had made and that time had discolored and darkened. "Grandpa."

"Yeah?" He didn't turn from the set, even though he had seen the movie countless times.

"I'm sorry."

"About what?"

"About letting you down."

Malcolm drew his attention away from the screen and gave Jacki a surprised look. "What the hell are you babbling about? You haven't let me down, Jak. You're a fighter. You've got more guts in your little finger than that worthless brother of yours."

She thought of her brother's house in an exclusive neighborhood of Newport Beach. "Caleb's worth a heck of a lot more than I am."

"Not in my book."

But she still wasn't convinced. "Maybe if I took Frank up on his proposal—I mean, I know he'd give us the money then and—"

The look her grandfather gave her made the words die on her lips. "Do you love him?"

She looked at her hands. "No, of course not, but—"

"But you'd do it for the ranch, and for me."

Jacki raised her head. "Yes."

Instead of being grateful, the words made him angry. He'd seen the love shining in her eyes. "Just what do you take me for, girl?"

"What?"

"Do you think I'd sell my own granddaughter for the ranch? You're my flesh and blood. I love this old place, but it's not the same as you." He reached over and patted her hand. For a moment warmth shimmered between them before he sat back and straightened his shoulders. "Now, if I could sell Caleb..."

She grinned. The mood had passed. "You wouldn't get enough."

"Enough? I wouldn't get anything, if the world had any sense." He poked a stubby finger toward the television. "I think you need to watch this movie more than I do. Jimmy Stewart doesn't think he's worth much, either, until that funny-looking angel shows him what life would be like without him. Empty."

"Now that's what I need." Jacki leaned forward and rested her chin on her knuckles. "An angel."

Malcolm crunched down another handful of chips before he commented. "Seems to me you've already got one, wholesale."

"What are you talking about?"

He tossed his head in the direction of the bunkhouse. "Gabriel. Good name for an angel."

Jacki laughed at the preposterous thought. "He's not an angel." No angel could make me feel what I just did tonight, she added silently.

Malcolm eyed her. There was no smile on his lips. "Found him in church, didn't you?"

She couldn't tell if he was putting her on or not. "Grandpa—"

"That's what's wrong with this younger generation," Malcolm muttered, half to himself, half to her. "Nobody knows how to believe anymore."

Jacki came around and hugged him, laughing. "I only wish he were, Grandpa. I only wish he were."

"Stop choking me and sit down and watch the movie." Malcolm shrugged himself free of her hold. "You might learn something."

His tone didn't fool her. "Yes, Grandpa." She grinned and took her place on the sofa.

Chapter Four

She had never had to use an alarm clock in her life. Jacki had an inner clock that woke her each morning without fail at four-thirty. Even as a child, unlike her twin, she had always been an early riser. It came in handy, living on the ranch. Work usually started before dawn's early light found her. There never seemed to be enough time to do everything. And "everything" seemed to be multiplying at a frightening rate in the past few months.

Jacki sat up in bed and stretched. Her sudden movement brought a low growl of complaint from the large, furry lump that lay next to her. She laughed softly as she reached over and scratched him behind the ear. The growl changed to the low sound of contentment.

"C'mon, Sweetheart. We've had enough beauty sleep. Time to get this ranch rolling." She sighed as she swung her legs out, placing her feet on the light gray carpet. "Or in this case, hobbling."

The Border collie yelped again. Whether in agreement or argument, Jacki had no idea. But he was at her feet before she stood up.

"That's the spirit, Sweetheart."

Jacki gave in and stretched one last time. A yawn followed and she halfheartedly stifled it. She was vaguely aware of an ache beginning to build behind her right temple, but disregarded it, hoping it wasn't what she thought it was.

"I certainly hope that the new hand follows your lead, Sweetheart."

The new hand. The words made Jacki smile. Yesterday afternoon the world had been painted completely in oppressive black. There had been absolutely no hope, nowhere to turn. Her time had been running out and all the hands had left. Now the black had turned to shades of gray. Maybe colors were on the horizon next, like dawn. Like a new start, she thought, absently rubbing her temple. Maybe this was the turning point, and things would start going right, for a change, from here on in. Lord knows, she mused, I'm certainly due.

"Speaking of due," Jacki announced aloud to the dog, who was poking at one of her boots with his nose, "I'm due in the kitchen."

Jacki looked at the blue silk teddy she slept in. The feel of silk against her skin was the one luxury she allowed herself. Somehow it helped negate the roughness of the land and the work she had to face each day.

"But not like this. Or he just might think that our bargain included something more than just pancakes for breakfast."

Sweetheart barked his answer.

"Easy for you to say," Jacki told him, tossing the words over her shoulder as she hurried into the bathroom for a two-minute shower. Turning her head cost her. The ache behind her temple throbbed a little harder. She remembered to grab her robe without missing a beat as she made her way out of the bathroom.

By five o'clock she was in the kitchen, her hair still damp from the quick shower. The dull pain in her temple continued to grow. It had the makings of a full-fledged migraine. She began to prepare breakfast with slow, deliberate moves, intent on moving her head as little as possible.

Malcolm directed his wheelchair toward the doorway, content for a moment to watch her as she moved about the kitchen. It stirred a warm, distant memory within him. Behind Jacki the table was already set. The sound of coffee, still perking, echoed within the kitchen, accompanying the sizzling noises coming from the griddle. She wore her grandmother's oversize apron over her faded jeans and work shirt. Forty years ago, Malcolm thought, his Ellen had looked like that.

She worked too damn hard, Malcolm thought as he maneuvered the wheelchair into the kitchen. The familiar thought was accompanied by the customary pang of guilt. He shifted his bulk uncomfortably in the chair and leaned over. Jacki's body blocked his line of vision.

"What's that I smell?" Unable to see, he angled his chair until he was on her left.

"Pancakes." Jacki glanced at him before turning her attention back to the griddle. A sharp pain etched itself on her eye and was gone. "Might have known the smell of food would bring you out." Carefully, systematically, she flipped three large, round pancakes over. The tops were golden brown. She smiled her satisfaction.

Malcolm raised a shaggy brow, noting the pained smile. "For me?"

"Among others." She lowered the flame, then silently counted to ten before taking the pancakes off, one at a time.

Malcolm watched her as she spooned more batter onto the griddle. He brushed back his beard from his lips in preparation. "I take it our new hand is still with us."

"He'd better be."

Feigning disinterest, she flipped the new pancakes over. Every movement was beginning to hurt and came echoing back to her in haunting stereo. Oh, no, not today, she thought miserably. I've got too much to do today.

Malcolm propelled his wheelchair backward until he was up against the kitchen table. He studied his granddaughter a moment as she moved the serving platter closer to his side. "Seems to me that you've taken a liking to him." He helped himself to the pancakes as Jacki brought over the second batch.

Jacki rested a hand on her hip and raised her brow. He was baiting her. Or maybe hoping. Lately their conversations were turning more and more to the subject of his seeing great-grandchildren before he died. "Leave some for him, okay?"

"Aha."

She lowered her face to his, even though it hurt to do so. "No aha! about it. I said I'd make him pancakes for breakfast, and I like keeping my word." She held up her hand to curtail any further discussion. "And as to your observation, I'd take a shine to the Hunchback of Notre Dame, if he promised to work for just meals and a roof over his head."

"He's not hard on the eyes, though, is he?" Malcolm commented slyly. He poured a pool of syrup on top of his pancakes.

"No," she admitted. "That he is not." She turned, to see Gabriel standing just outside the kitchen doorway. She felt color rising to her face. Oh, God, how much had he heard?

Acting as if there were nothing in the conversation to utterly embarrass his granddaughter, Malcolm turned to give Gabriel a long look. The white whiskers parted to frame a very satisfied smile. His first impression hadn't been a hasty one. He still felt strongly that this one was going to work out. Maybe in a number of ways.

"Pull up a chair, boy." He gestured with his fork. "We were just talking about you."

Jacki wondered if her grandfather had thought to see fit to build a trapdoor in the kitchen. Preferably one in working order and directly beneath her feet. Her headache threaten to overpower her.

"So I understood." Gabriel nodded at Jacki before he took a chair opposite Malcolm. "I knocked," he explained, "but no one heard."

Jacki closed her eyes for a moment, wishing her mortification and her headache away. Neither disappeared. Then she looked accusingly at Sweetheart. The dog always barked loudly enough to rattle the dishes whenever someone approached, even someone he knew. "Some watchdog you are."

Malcolm held his coffee cup toward Jacki. "He's not supposed to protect us from our hands, Jak." Hot, thick liquid filled his cup to the rim, sending up a swirl of steam before he withdrew it.

"That never stopped him before." She moved the well-worn coffeepot toward Gabriel and gestured at his empty cup. "Coffee?"

Quickly he brought his cup to meet the pot as she tilted it. "Please." Then he smiled at her. Slowly. Fully.

It filled every single vacancy she felt within her, like the first rays of the morning sun on a darkened land. Staring, Jacki nearly poured too much into his cup. To her everlasting relief she caught herself in time. For her effort, the headache spread to encompass both her temples and traveled halfway up her skull. She was doomed, she thought in despair. It was going to be one of those days.

Gabriel looked at the serving platter. "Pancakes." An almost sensuous delight was audible in the single word. It had been too long, he thought. For a moment he savored the sight, then helped himself to the top two pancakes.

Jacki grinned despite her mounting pain. "I promised." Why should pancakes mean that much to him?

"Not everyone keeps their promises." He reached for the syrup.

Jacki pushed the syrup and butter toward him, unconsciously wincing as she did so. "I do." She heard Malcolm mutter a complaint. "You have enough," she said matter-of-factly, glancing at his plate. The doctor had warned her about letting Malcolm eat too much, and she intended to see that he kept his weight under control, even if it earned her a few choice comments.

Gabriel raised his eyes to her momentarily. A woman who always keeps her word. Another rare attribute. The tally was mounting. "That's good to know."

His tone, more than anything else, caught her attention. Jacki couldn't help but feel that there was always more to Gabriel's simple words than was evident on the surface. She shook the feeling from her, telling herself that the stress of the situation was getting to her. That— and the building migraine that was fighting for possession of her head. There were no hidden messages. Gabriel was simply a cowboy, one she knew she had been fabulously lucky to find.

Bringing over a third platter of pancakes, Jacki took her place between the two men, leaving her own plate empty as they ate. Instead she poured herself a cup of steaming coffee. After taking a perfunctory sip of the black liquid, she placed the cup against her aching forehead. The heat helped, but not much.

Gabriel noticed the slightly pained look around her eyes, the tense jawline and wondered if she was ill. "You're not eating?"

She was surprised both by his show of concern and by the simple fact that he was actually asking a question. Maybe there was hope for him, after all. She shrugged carelessly, then slowly moved the coffee cup back and forth above her eyes. "I'm not hungry."

"She's got another one of her headaches," Malcolm volunteered.

Though they were few and far between, he knew the signs. They came early and lasted a day or two. This, too, he blamed himself for. The burden of being responsible for the ranch did this to her. Part of Malcolm felt that he should finally sell the ranch and be done with it—and with dreams of the past that refused to materialize again. It was selfish of him not to spare her this heavy responsibility. And yet he couldn't bring himself to do it. For him it would be like turning his back on his whole life.

"Grandpa," Jacki warned softly. "Gabriel isn't interested in my headaches."

Gabriel leaned back in his chair and studied her face for a long moment. "Take anything for it?"

Embarrassed by suddenly being the center of attention, Jacki scooped up her grandfather's plate and placed it upon her empty one as she rose.

Malcolm made a pretense of trying to get it back. "Hey, I'm not finished yet," he grumbled.

She leaned over and patted his stomach. "Oh, yes, you are." Then, because she knew he was waiting for an answer, she looked toward Gabriel. "And no, I'm not taking anything for it. Nothing helps, anyway. Thank you for your concern, but it'll wear itself out. In a day or two," she added, the last words spoken under her breath.

Gabriel picked up his own plate and cup and followed her to the sink. He placed the items on the counter, then opened the door on his left. "Do you mind?" He nodded toward the pantry.

He had eaten three rather large pancakes. Was he still hungry? "No, help yourself."

Keeping her curiosity in check, she looked away as he rummaged quietly. With slow determination she began to wash the breakfast dishes. Last night's had been washed, but they were still sitting on the rack, waiting to be put away. She had promised herself to clear the kitchen before she went on to the chores outside. On days like today she missed having Maria around. It would have been nice not to have to worry about every single detail that went into running a household. But there was no point in wishing for things that couldn't be. Just hanging on to the ranch was good enough for her at the moment.

Malcolm drained the last drop of coffee that Jacki allowed him to have until lunch. Cup met saucer with a resounding note of contact. It echoed in Jacki's head. "Well, if you two'll excuse me, there's some technical reading I wanted to catch up on in my room." Pushing the chair back from the table, Malcolm wheeled himself out of the kitchen.

Sweetheart sat on the floor between Jacki and Gabriel, thumping his tail on the linoleum like a noisy, furry metronome. He was waiting for a handout. This morning the thumping sounded inordinately loud to her. She pursed her lips as she leaned over his bowl and told herself she wasn't dizzy.

"Just fresh water and one piece, hear?" She held one of the remaining pancakes in front of the dog. "It's not good for you. Between Sweetheart and Grandpa," she said to Gabriel, still looking at the Border collie, "I seem to say that a lot around here."

The pancake was snatched before she had a chance to place it in his bowl. Sweetheart stood with his head cocked, still looking expectantly at Jacki, his pink tongue working the edges of his mouth, where the syrup had smeared itself.

Jacki straightened, her hand automatically going to her forehead. She tried willing the arrow that was piercing her skull to disappear. Her eyes felt as if they were going to bulge out of her head. What a day to pick to feel this way. She sighed. Actually there were no easy days on the ranch anymore.

Taking a step back, she bumped against Gabriel. Turning took effort. She was aware of small, inviting sparks licking through her as her body came into contact with his, but the sparks were extinguished by the thudding pain. This was going to turn into a wasted day any moment now, and she didn't have time to waste.

"Here."

Jacki opened her eyes and looked at an opaque glass of foaming something-or-other that Gabriel held out to her.

"What?" She eyed it as suspiciously as she could manage under the circumstances.

"Drink it." It was an order covered in velvet, but an order, nonetheless.

Jacki looked at the lean, darkly dressed cowboy, the ache spreading to her neck. Her shoulders would be next, she thought, and then she'd be utterly incapacitated. Damn it, anyway. "Why would I want to do that?"

"It'll make your headache go away."

Bubbles were rising above the rim and bursting gently, sprinkling a light spray onto his hand. "It looks like something the witch gave Sleeping Beauty to make her sleep for a hundred years."

Gabriel grinned easily, but she noticed that he didn't put the glass down. "I think you have your fairy tales mixed up."

Jacki took the glass from him gingerly, feeling oddly game. It was cold and wet in her hand. The fizz looked as if it would never stop. "What's in it?"

His eyes held hers. "A little of this, a little of that."

She remembered his answer when she'd asked him where he had worked. "Here and there," he had answered. Vague, always so vague. Why? "Don't you ever get specific?"

Her head continued to pound. The pain was jabbing at her shoulders. What did it matter if he was vague? Maybe this magic potion would help. Right now the ache was so bad, she'd have sold her soul to the devil to get some kind of relief.

"Sometimes it's a lot simpler not to." Gently he nudged the glass toward her mouth, his fingers on hers. "It'll make you feel better. I promise."

It was the look in his eyes more than his hypnotic tone of voice that convinced her. Besides, how bad could it be? He had concocted the brew, using things that came from her own pantry. There was nothing in there that could do her any more harm than the migraine was already accomplishing.

"The only thing that'll make me feel better right now is a new head."

But she sipped the brew, anyway. It tasted extremely bitter and strange. She thought she detected a touch of lemon, but the other tastes were foreign to her, as if they were all masking one another. The fizz tickled her nose and glazed her cheeks as she took a deep sip. Hoping she satisfied him, she offered the glass to Gabriel.

But he didn't take it from her. Instead he shook his head. "The whole thing."

Wondering if her stomach could stand a second attack, Jacki brought the glass back to her lips and drained it. She shivered as she placed the glass on the counter. She felt as if her whole body had been involved in drinking this foul-tasting liquid.

"That had to be one of the worst things I've ever had," Jacki pronounced.

Gabriel took the glass and rinsed it out before he answered her. "It's not meant to taste good. It's meant to cure your headache."

"You accomplish that and you're a miracle worker," she said with a soft laugh that didn't seem to hurt her head as much as she'd anticipated. Gabriel said nothing in reply, only smiled. Back to normal, she thought. She looked down at Sweetheart, who had shifted to stand at Gabriel's side. Well, not quite back to normal, she amended. The dog seemed to have adopted him.

Mechanically Jacki took the glass from the drain board and dried it. "So what time do your friends get up in the morning?" She hung the damp dish towel on a magnetic hook on the refrigerator. Her words were met with a slightly puzzled expression. "I thought we'd pick up your horse first thing. You said you were boarding it with your friends," she reminded him, vaguely wondering if perhaps that had been said in order to save face. After all, the man seemed to have nothing else to call his own. Maybe he'd needed the lie of saying he owned a horse.

No, she decided abruptly, Gabriel Goodfellow didn't need any sort of lies to see him through. He seemed to have that larger-than-life presence about him that didn't make a person think about what sort of worldly goods the man owned. He was a loner, a rugged man. A survivor. Possessions weren't important.

In the background, from the living room, Malcolm's old grandfather clock chimed six times. "They should be up by the time we get there. Their place is just outside of San Clemente."

It sounded suspiciously like a guarantee, Jacki thought as she took off the apron she was wearing and folded it carefully, before placing it on the first shelf in the pantry.

Gabriel watched her and thought that the apron had to have some sentimental value for her. "Your mother's?" He nodded at the apron.

Jacki closed the pantry's double doors. "My grandmother's. Makes me feel as if I could cook up a feast when I wear it." Jacki led the way into the living room. She noticed that the door to the den stood ajar. A whiff of smoke was barely detectable. She shook her head. Had to be watched every minute.

"It was."

Jacki turned around to look at Gabriel, her thoughts interrupted. "Was what?"

His face was just inches away from hers, and he curbed an ancient desire. In all his travels he had never seen a more sensually attractive face. There was no powder adorning the slender, high cheekbones, no eyeshadow tinting the lids of the almond-shaped eyes, only a touch of gloss on her full lips. But it was more than enough to stir a man and remind him of the more basic needs that had once been part of his life. He brought his mind back to the conversation. "A feast."

"Pancakes?"

"Pancakes."

"No smoking, Grandpa!" she shouted over her shoulder as she moved toward the front door.

"Man can't do nothing in his own home," she heard him grumble and tried not to laugh. She looked at Gabriel. "You're easily satisfied." Jacki reached for her jacket on the hook by the door.

"It's been a long, long time since I've eaten pancakes."

She stopped, her hand on her jacket. He didn't look like a helpless man. At the very least he'd make them for himself, if he wanted them. Of that she felt sure. "Where have you been?"

He didn't look as if he would answer her for a moment, which made her wonder all the more. And then, when he opened his mouth, the answer was familiar.

"Up—"

"North," she completed with a laugh and a shake of her head. A man of mystery through and through. She was going to have to come to terms with that. She didn't like mysteries. She liked knowing. Everything. A born snoop, her grandfather had called her.

Jacki stepped onto the porch, shoving her hands deep into her pockets. Above her, the last traces of stars were fading away, having lost their competition with the breathtaking hues of the rising sun. The morning air was cold and bracing against her cheeks. It felt wonderful just to be alive.

"C'mon, the Jeep's over here." On impulse, she threaded her arm through Gabriel's and led him around the side of the house.

Feeling a tiny pinch of regret, Jacki dropped her hand from his arm as they separated at the Jeep. She walked over to the driver's side. He sat down silently next to her, as silently, she thought, as a morning shadow. She turned the key in the ignition and let the car warm up a moment before she threw it into Drive. "You're going to have to give me directions on how to get there."

Gabriel nodded. "No problem." He turned slightly in his seat. "By the way."

He's actually going to start a conversation. Will wonders never cease. "Yes?"

"How's your headache?"

"It's—" She paused suddenly, then turned to look at him, stunned. "Gone." The word was whispered, shrouded in surprise.

Gabriel said nothing as he leaned back in his seat. He smiled.

Jacki was speechless as she turned her eyes back to the road. The man had performed nothing short of a miracle, one that had eluded all the prominent pharmaceutical companies. As she drove toward the rising sun, a myriad of questions filled the corners of her mind—a mind that had been filled with pain only a short while ago.

Chapter Five

It felt good to be working on his own again, to be doing something solid. Something productive. Gabriel had spent too much of his time feeling useless. He had had to banish his love of life's small pleasures to the recesses of his mind. To dwell on what was unobtainable would have been unbearable. Now he was here again. Touching the earth, smelling the early-morning dew, watching the sun rise. Eating pancakes, he grinned.

Time to stop daydreaming and get back to work.

With very little effort he shook the past from his mind. He had gotten good at that, Gabriel thought with satisfaction. Good at ridding his mind of anything troublesome or disconcerting. He was here now, being useful, helping someone. And helping himself, as well. He couldn't ask for anything more.

He whistled softly as he spread new hay along the stall with his pitchfork. Even the tedious chore of mucking out the stalls felt good to him.

Jacki felt a jab in the palm of her hand and stopped to examine it. A tiny, brown sliver of wood protruded slightly. Carefully she plucked it out, then rubbed her hand along the back of her jeans, dispelling the sting. Fortunes of war, she thought.

A low tune caught her attention just as she went back to work. Jacki stopped and leaned on the handle of the shovel. The melody was hauntingly stirring, making her feel inexplicably happy. She had been working at the opposite end of the stable from Gabriel. Outside, the eight horses she and her grandfather owned were meandering about in the corral, waiting to be returned to their stalls.

Intrigued, Jacki watched Gabriel as he spread the hay around the last stall. Though she considered herself a fast worker, Gabriel was doing two stalls to her one. Just as he had yesterday. And the day before that.

He obviously didn't mind hard work. On the contrary, he seemed to thrive on it. He obviously liked working around horses. And his interaction with Sweetheart hadn't been a fluke. He was good with all animals. Her own mares, so skittish in the new condition they found themselves in, responded to his gentle touch, to the sound of his voice.

Just, she thought with a smile, as all living things seemed to.

Just as she did.

She caught his eye. "I've never heard anyone whistling while they cleaned out the horse stalls before," she called to him. "Most of the hands we've had at Los Caballos have tried to save their breath in here."

She wrinkled her own nose as she said it. She loved ranching, had always thought that horses were the most beautiful of all God's creatures, but the smell of a stable had never held any poetic allure for her.

He gave her one of those grins that affected her more and more each time she was on the receiving end. Jacki wondered if he knew.

"It's all in how you look at things." The stalls on his end finished, Gabriel crossed to her side. "Need any help finishing up?" He put out his hand for her shovel. They could hear the mares and the geldings in the corral getting restless.

Jacki released her shovel with a tinge both of guilt and pleasure. "I never turn down a helping hand." She stepped back to allow him room in the stall. She knew she should begin bringing the mares in, but she wanted to talk to Gabriel for a moment. She knew so little about this man who had so quickly become part of her life. "And how do you look at things?"

His back was to her as he shoveled yesterday's hay into the buckets they had brought in. "As a rule, optimistically."

She wondered why. He didn't seem to have anything or anyone except the horse they had brought back with them the first morning. It seemed to her that it would be a little difficult to nurture optimism under those conditions. He was so different from anyone she had ever met. What made him the way he was? Since he had arrived last week, each day raised more questions in her mind about him. More questions and no answers.

"Really?"

He paused in his work to look at her. He knew that there were things he should tell her, things she'd want to know. But for now they would have to keep. If it was right he could tell her later, when he felt sure that she could understand.

The bright, morning sun shone in through the open stable door, bathing him in light. It was a contrast to the dark shirt and jeans he wore. The sun highlighted his bronzed skin and made him seem almost golden. Almost—the thought flittered quickly through Jacki's mind—as if he weren't of this world.

"Really."

"Why?" she persisted, wanting to know his reasons. She was basically optimistic herself. If she hadn't been, she would have given up long ago. But at least she had a basis for it, a past. He seemed to be a drifter. Was he? And if he was, what made a drifter see things in a hopeful light? What made *him* see things the way he did? She had a sudden hunger to know.

"Why not?" he countered easily.

She felt a little self-conscious at asking. With a small shrug she ran her hand through her dark hair, pushing it back from her eyes. She pulled a bandanna out of her pocket and secured her hair away from her face.

"You know, Gabriel, if you ever decide not to be a ranch hand, you could always become a psychiatrist. They have the annoying habit of answering questions with questions, too."

She turned to return Blue Belle to her stall. The sound of his voice stopped her and robbed her of the cloak of annoyance. Slowly she turned and looked at him over her shoulder.

"I didn't mean to annoy you," he said quietly. His deep blue eyes moved unhurriedly over her face, touching her, communicating. And Jacki knew he was telling her the truth.

She shook her head, a tinge of embarrassment licking her insides. "Sorry." She laughed, toying with the bridle that she held in her hand for Blue Belle. "I ask too many questions."

He liked the sound of her laughter. It made him think of drops of gentle spring rain falling on newly sprouted green leaves. It made him think of springtime. And hope. "And I don't answer enough."

"No, you don't," she agreed honestly. "But maybe we'll work that out."

He leaned the shovel against the stall and took hold of the pitchfork. "Maybe." He went back to work in earnest. There were many more chores waiting for him before he could call it a day.

There was no "maybe" about it, Jacki decided. Come hell or high water, she was going to learn things about Mr. Gabriel Goodfellow, whether he wanted her to or not. Her curiosity was aroused—along with something else, if she was being honest.

She looked and saw that though he was working at a steady pace, Gabriel was watching her from beneath those dark lashes of his. She suddenly felt as if he could see right into her mind and read her thoughts. Even if he could, that wasn't going to stop her.

"I'll bring the horses back in while you finish up," she told him.

He merely nodded.

"That for him?" Malcolm asked, eyeing the thick, roast beef sandwich Jacki was putting together.

Jacki had learned long ago not to be startled when her grandfather came up behind her. For a stocky man, he had always moved rather lightly on his feet. What never ceased to amaze her was that now that he was in a wheelchair, he still managed to be quiet when he approached.

She plopped a large leaf of lettuce over the mayonnaise and closed the work of art with the second piece of bread. There, that should hold him.

"He's not coming in for lunch today, and he forgot to take something with him," she told Malcolm casually as she wrapped the sandwich. Moving aside a container of orange juice, she placed the sandwich next to its mate in the basket. "He's still mending breaks in the fence. I thought I'd drive over and bring it to him."

"Thoughtful." Malcolm stroked his beard and made no effort to hide the smile that spread apart the white whiskers about his mouth.

Jacki sighed. The old man had a one-track mind. She stepped to the refrigerator, and Sweetheart danced away from her feet, a moment before he tripped his mistress. But Jacki's mind was on her grandfather, not the collie. "Don't give me that knowing look of yours, Grandpa. I did promise him food."

He drew slowly on his pipe and exhaled, watching a smoke ring form. "Yup. That you did." His tone told her exactly what he thought of her excuse.

Jacki waved the smoke ring away with an impatient hand. "Doctor doesn't like you smoking that."

"And I don't like the doctor, so we're even." Defiantly he took another pull on his meerschaum pipe, then studied the purple- and brown-streaked white bowl with its intricate carvings. He could remember when his wife had given him that. On their twentieth anniversary. Their last anniversary. Jacki needed memories such as that, he thought helplessly. "How's he working out?"

Jacki shoved a handful of napkins into the basket. "Gabriel?"

"Yes, Gabriel. I already know how the doctor's working out. Damn poorly." Malcolm rubbed his numbed legs and grumbled under his breath.

Jacki felt a shaft of pity sting her, but let it pass. Pity was something Malcolm wouldn't tolerate from anyone, not even from her. He was too proud for that. Better the bantering words and one-upmanship that went on between them. He enjoyed trading barbs, not garnering sympathy. Never that. "You can't expect miracles, Grandpa."

He let the pipe go out. "I can expect anything I damn well please, missy. Now I asked you how Gabriel was turning out. This is still my ranch, and standing or sitting, I still run things."

As an afterthought she opened the refrigerator again and hunted out a cold apple. Sweetheart growled as she put it into the basket, out of his reach. "No one ever said any differently."

Malcolm tapped the dead pipe against the arm of his chair. "I didn't mean to snap, Jak."

She stopped and looked at him. This was as close as he came to an apology, and she wasn't one to milk it. "I know you didn't." She kissed the top of his head. "You're just ornery, that's all. And to answer your question—" She snapped down the lid on her picnic basket, deliberately moving it to the center of the table, away from the collie. "He's working out just fine. We couldn't have gotten a better hand if we had stolen him."

He had expected no less. Malcolm chuckled knowingly. "Maybe he's working so hard because he has his eye on the boss's granddaughter."

I wish, she thought, but kept the sentiment to herself. This was no time for romance. She had the ranch's survival to think of.

"The only thing Gabriel has his eye on, bless him, is work." In the last two weeks she had caught what she thought might have been an appreciative glance or two cast in her direction, but had decided that it was probably just wishful thinking on her part.

Malcolm was unconvinced. "Doesn't strike me as a stupid boy."

Her jacket was hanging on the back of a kitchen chair. She picked it up and slung it over her shoulder. With her free hand she took hold of the picnic basket. "He's not." She bent to give Malcolm another quick kiss, this time on the cheek. His beard tickled her chin. "Why on earth would he want you as an in-law?" With a gay, light-hearted laugh, Jacki sauntered out.

He gripped the arms of his chair in order to lean over better. "A whole bunch of reasons," Malcolm called after her.

"I'll give you until this evening to come up with one," she retorted, throwing the words over her shoulder before she let the outer door close behind her.

Sweetheart yelped as the door almost caught his tail. Bounding down the front steps, he danced about her eagerly, then ran for the Jeep. With a leap he positioned himself in the passenger's seat. Jacki pushed the picnic basket onto the floor in front of the back seat.

"No passengers this time, Sweetheart. Besides, you're supposed to be Grandpa's dog, remember? Go keep him company." The dog remained sitting in the passenger's seat. "Now."

With a rumbling growl the Border collie leaped off the seat.

"You're beginning to sound more like Grandpa every day, dog. Now mind me." She watched the dog take exactly one step back. He stopped and eyed her. So much for obedience. "See you later." With one hand on the wheel, she turned the Jeep and headed toward the north pasture.

The lighthearted feeling within her began to grow stronger, and Jacki sang along with the tune that the deejay was playing on her radio.

She saw him in the distance, a lone figure working on a broken section of fence. The day was unseasonably warm, and he had stripped to the waist. A sheen of sweat glistened on his shoulders and back. She watched his muscles tense and ripple. Something inside Jacki stirred, then tightened like a coiled spring. She felt her heart begin to drum just a little harder than it had been doing before.

"Face it, Jak, you're falling for the hired help," she murmured as she approached.

No, he'd never be that. He might work for his keep, but he'd never be anyone's "hired help." There was something too noble about him, she thought. Dressed in rags, he would still have exuded it. He was his own man, not anyone else's, no matter what the circumstances.

Gabriel heard her approaching in the Jeep long before he stopped working. Even if she hadn't been driving, he would have heard her. He was becoming attuned to the vibrations she gave off. Turning now, he rubbed the sweat from his brow with the back of his hand. "Almost finished." He let the hammer in his hand drop into the circle of tools on the ground.

"So I see."

Gabriel let his eyes skim over Jacki. Even driving the Jeep, she moved like a thoroughbred, he thought, with a smooth, flowing rhythm like the horses she adored. Suddenly he felt a hunger gnawing at him that had nothing to do with food. It was surprising that feelings that had been dormant for so long could flourish, he mused. It was like riding a bicycle. You never really forgot how.

He knew he shouldn't allow this feeling to grow. But her very presence nurtured it. He had never thought that temptation was good for the soul, either. Temptation was his version of hell. The thought made him smile absently.

What's he thinking about? she wondered. His smile looked so mysterious. Maybe he thought she was here to make sure he was working.

"I wasn't coming to check up on you."

The look on his face told her he knew that. It seemed to her that he knew everything moments before she said it. An annoying habit, if he weren't so terribly appealing. And he was that—very, very appealing. The strong, silent type, she thought. It actually existed.

Jacki cleared her throat. "I brought you your lunch. You forgot it."

He ran his hand over his belly. The muscles were taut, the result of hard work and care. His worn, faded jeans were slung tightly on slim hips. Jacki told herself that her thoughts had definitely veered away from the safe path and upbraided herself for it—but not with as much force as she could have.

"My stomach was starting to grumble, but I was trying to ignore it." He dropped his hand from his stomach and took the picnic basket.

"I'm sorry. I should have come out sooner." She began to climb out of the Jeep and was surprised when he took her hand to help her out. Standing on the ground, she found herself only an inch away from him. She could feel the heat of his body, could smell the perspiration his labors had generated. Her breath caught in her throat.

"That's all right, Jacki. I've been hungry before."

She almost shook her head to clear it. Scarlet flashes of fire spread all through her, licking at her insides. Her palms became damp. This was something very new to her.

"Not while you work here." She breathed deeply, slowly, in order to steady her voice. She felt tongue-tied around him. Tongue-tied, as if she were treading on unsure ground. She had never felt that way around a man before. It struck her again how unlike anyone else he was.

Being too outspoken for her own good was her problem, her grandfather had said. Yet Gabriel made her feel shy. It was as if she were in the presence of someone too good to be true. And utterly, utterly mysterious. She still hadn't gotten him to tell her what he had put into that drink he had concocted to cure her headache, where he was originally from, or any one of a host of questions that ran through her mind.

"We had a bargain, remember?"

"I always remember bargains, but not everyone else does." Gabriel opened the picnic basket and looked into it. "There's more than enough here for me." He let the lid fall again as he looked at her.

"Is that an invitation or a criticism of my wastefulness?" She bit her lip. That, she told herself, was really reaching. She was honest enough to be ashamed of herself. "I'm sorry."

"For what?" He seemed not to understand her meaning. Or pretended not to, she thought gratefully. "I'm the one who's lacking in manners. Join me? Or is there something you have to do?"

She thought of several "somethings," all of which two weeks ago would have been labeled as important, if not downright urgent. Now nothing seemed quite as earth-shattering anymore.

"Nothing that won't keep for a little while." She nodded toward the Jeep. "Why don't we sit in the Jeep? That way we can enjoy the food without help from the insects."

He slipped on his shirt, and she felt a tinge of regret. She told herself she was being foolish. She was beginning to act like a love-struck teen, and at twenty-six she was far from that. But had she ever been love-struck? she wondered suddenly. No, not to her recollection. She had totally bypassed that stage. Until now.

Gabriel didn't bother buttoning his shirt. He'd only have to take it off again after lunch. It hung open on either side of a smooth, muscular chest.

The sight of him sitting next to her like that unnerved her. It shouldn't, she told herself, but it did, nonetheless.

"You know," she said, peeling back the tinfoil from her sandwich, "you're working much too fast. At this rate we'll be out of things for you to do."

No, there would always be things to do, Jacki thought, settling back in the Jeep and yet unable to relax. But for some reason she needed to talk. Even now, when her sandwich was threatening to stick to the roof of her mouth, which had gone very, very dry.

Another man might have made a joke about perhaps finally getting paid for his work, or expressed concern for his job. Gabriel appeared merely to absorb the information. "Then I can get started on the house."

She remembered his comment when he had first come. The house did need work. There had never been enough time to do anything but temporary repairs on it. She had always hoped that there would be more time to do things right later on, when things went smoothly. But they hadn't gone smoothly for a while now.

"Grandpa would like that." Overhead a gaggle of geese called to one another as they flew in formation, their destination determined since the beginning of time. Nature at its best, she thought, sneaking a look at Gabriel. At its very best.

Gabriel leaned an elbow against the back of his seat as he ate. "This is a beautiful ranch, Jacki."

He couldn't have said anything to please her more. "I spent every summer here as a child. My very first memory is of Grandpa putting me on this mountain of a horse and leading me around the corral." She laughed softly. "It was actually a pony, but when you're three, everything's large. Especially your grandfather." She closed her eyes for a moment, remembering. "He was such a giant of a man to me, so alive, so robust."

Without realizing it, she'd relaxed, Gabriel noticed. Then he heard a hint of sadness enter her voice. "As time went on, I got bigger, he got smaller. But he's still bigger than life to me. Being confined to a wheelchair is really hard on him." He saw her eyes grow dark.

"He seems to be adjusting fairly well, though."

"He won't be if he has to sell the ranch."

"Tell me about the ranch, Jacki."

She felt as if she had known him forever and that there was no need to actually have to tell him things. Somehow he *knew*. But the words came anyway and with them, an inexplicable desire to say more. "There isn't that much to tell. It was big, now it's small."

"Why?"

His tone was soft, coaxing. Responses came easily. "Because of the mortgage."

He looked down thoughtfully at the empty foil in his hand. He balled it slowly. "I would have thought that a place this old would have paid off its mortgage a long time ago."

"It did. The first one. But after Caleb and I came to live with him, Grandpa took out another mortgage, so that we could have money to go to college." The guilt she always felt drove a new shaft through her now as she recounted the story. Had it not been for her, things might have been different.

"And?"

She shrugged. "We went. Caleb kept on going, I came home."

He liked the ring the word had and the way she said it. In the single word he heard all her feelings, knew all her values. It drew her closer to him. There was a bond there now, even though she didn't know it.

"Then what happened?"

Tears rose to her eyes—tears that always came with the memory. "And then we had to shoot Seawater, Grandpa's prize thoroughbred. Seawater broke his leg, and there was absolutely no hope for him. No hope." Her throat felt dry. She took a deep breath, then let it out slowly as she stared straight ahead. The geese had faded to a single speck in the sky. "It seemed as if everything went wrong after that. Grandpa had to sell off pieces of the ranch, and then he had that accident at the fair three years ago."

She squeezed her eyes shut and saw it all happening again. She felt Gabriel's hand on hers and realized that she had clenched her hand into a fist. She opened her eyes and one by one, released her fingers, but not so far that they would lose contact with him. She could feel that odd sensation of strength coming back to her, strength that seemed to radiate from him.

"It was at the competition. One minute Grandpa was riding the mustang, determined to prove he still had what it took to tame a wild spirit. The next, he was sailing through the air.'' Her heart pounded as she spoke. The moment had been frozen in time for her. ''And then he came down, hitting the ground and lying there like a limp doll. A broken, limp doll. There were a dozen doctors after that, therapists, endless tests and X rays, and a mountain of bills to see to. More pieces of the ranch went.''

She straightened her shoulders, as if facing it all over again. ''The doctors were very kind, but the words had all been the same. He wouldn't walk. Not ever again.'' She looked into Gabriel's eyes and knew without being told that he understood the anguish. ''The fall hadn't killed him, but the prognosis almost did.'' She licked her lower lip. ''Somehow, though, he had come through because I willed it, because I refused to let him die.''

Gabriel nodded. He knew the power of positive thinking. It had gotten him through, when there had been nothing but emptiness to face. It had helped him not to give up.

''And Grandpa decided to go on. For me. I also know that he went on, *is* going on, because he believes that somewhere around the corner there is a miracle with his name on it.''

She stopped suddenly and laughed dryly. How had he gotten her to talk about all this, when she couldn't even get him to tell her what was in a fizzing glass of cloudy water?

''Maybe there is.''

There was something in his voice that made her want to believe, to cling to that herself. ''I'd really like to believe that.''

Gabriel let the foil drop into the basket and closed the lid. His eyes held hers. ''Then believe it. Miracles only happen when you believe.''

Make me believe, Gabriel. I need to believe. "You sound like you have experience with that."

"Some."

She opened her mouth to say something else, but he got out of the Jeep abruptly. "Well, I'd better be getting back. There's another fence post I have to dig. Thanks for bringing lunch."

She stared after him, thinking about his last words. Would he ever answer any of her questions? She was beginning to doubt it. But it didn't change her reaction to him. She started the Jeep. "Anytime, Gabriel. I'll see you at dinner."

He turned around for only a moment. "I'll be there."

Jacki sang all the way back to the ranch house.

Chapter Six

Jacki hurried into the kitchen, running half an hour behind schedule. She was winded. It seemed to her that
lately she was always behind schedule, even with Gabriel
helping. She upbraided herself for spending so much time
exercising the horses this afternoon, but because of the
picnic lunch she had shared with Gabriel, her mood had
been indulgent. And now, she thought, glancing at the
kitchen clock, she had to pay the piper. She shrugged out
of her jacket and tossed it carelessly over the back of the
kitchen chair as she reached for her grandmother's apron
in the pantry and opened the refrigerator at the same
time.

Slipping the apron's loop over her head, she pulled the
ends of her dark hair free and wondered dismally if what
she was engaged in what was basically just rearranging
deck chairs on the *Titanic*. All this work they were putting in, all these "business as usual" motions she was
going through, were they all futile? Would the bank wind

up holding the reins to the ranch by the beginning of the year? Defiantly she wanted to yell no, but was too much of a realist to always be optimistic. An overwhelming feeling of dread washed over her.

The bank would own the ranch.

No!

She slammed a large cast-iron pot onto the counter. Jacki cringed at the cracking sound as pot met tile. Hoping against hope, she raised the pot and looked at the point of contact. There was a hair-thin, zigzag line running through the tile. She thought she was going to cry and knew it had little to do with the broken gray tile. Stifling a sob, she brushed away one hot tear with the back of her hand and forbade others to form.

Damn Caleb and his "business sense." Damn him for not having a heart. If he helped, if he gave back some of what he had gotten from their grandfather, then they'd be all right. They just needed to stay afloat until the spring, until the foals came and could be sold. A little time, a little luck, a lot of money. That was what was needed.

And that, she thought as she looked for the carrots in the bottom of the refrigerator, was just what she didn't have.

Sweetheart entered the kitchen, sniffing around as Jacki squatted on the floor, rummaging through the vegetable bin. He looked on with interest.

"Out of my way, dog. I'm behind schedule." Jacki yanked out a bag half-filled with carrots. "So what else is new, right?" she muttered, rising.

"Couldn't find him?"

She whipped around, startled. Her hand flew to her heart. This time her grandfather's entrance almost had her leaping out of her skin. Jumpy, she was getting jumpy. This down-to-the-wire situation with the ranch was really getting to her. Jacki took a deep breath. "What?"

Malcolm shifted his head to the right, studying her closely. "Gabriel. Last I saw you, you were heading out with lunch for the man. What's the matter? Couldn't you find him?"

She dumped all the carrots into the sink with a vengeance. She picked up one and began to scrape it. "Yes, I found him. Why?"

"Well, the way you're banging those pots around—" he jerked his thumb at the one on the counter "—I thought that maybe you found out that he ran off with the horses or was married to three women at the same time."

Jacki tried not to look guilty about the pot. She reached for the cutting board that hung on the wall next to the sink and began chopping methodically. "The horses are exactly where we left them, bless 'em, and why would I care if Gabriel had thirty wives, as long as he keeps working the way he has?" With a quick move of her wrist she brought the knife down—and very nearly cut off her finger.

She swallowed an oath. Steady, Jak, better to serve dinner late than end up with nine fingers.

Malcolm's eyes never left her as he reached for one of the carrot sticks that had as yet avoided her flying knife. He broke it in half and let Sweetheart dispose of one piece. "It's my legs that're bad, girl, not my eyes."

"You use glasses," she reminded him. Sweetheart raised his head to see what remained on the counter for his pleasure. Jacki glared at the dog as she went on with her preparations.

Malcolm snared a second piece of a carrot before she could deposit it with the rest in the pot on the stove. "For reading, not for seeing."

"Maybe you should get a pair for that, too," she retorted matter-of-factly. In her heart she didn't want her grandfather getting his hopes up. Gabriel had had plenty of opportunities to kiss her, and he hadn't. Maybe he wasn't interested in her. Maybe she just wasn't his type, after all.

But then if she *wasn't*, why did he watch her the way he did? There was interest in his eyes, she could almost swear to it. It was almost as if he wanted her, but couldn't allow himself to let go. As if, she thought, he had made some sort of vow to stay chaste. But that was silly, she thought. Only priests did that, and if he were a priest he would have told her.

"You're telling me you're not attracted to him?"

She turned, the last remaining carrot stick in her hand. As she spoke, she waved it for emphasis. Out of the corner of her eye she saw Sweetheart waiting for his chance. That dog would eat absolutely anything, she thought.

"I'm telling you that until the ranch is solvent, until Little Nell finds a way to save the homestead and foil Snively Whiplash by getting ahold of the deed, I don't have time to think of anything."

Which was a lie, she thought. She *was* thinking of Gabriel. Maybe that was the problem; maybe that was why she couldn't come up with a way to pay off the second trust deed. There *had* to be one, but she couldn't see it. She was preoccupied. But, damn it all, he was very attractive.

Unable to resist the orange baton any longer, Malcolm reached out and took the carrot stick from her hand. He took a healthy bite and chewed, his small, gray eyes on her. "Horse manure."

"Yes, there was plenty of that this morning, as there is every morning." Taking five small potatoes from the sack on the counter, she began to peel them slowly. "Can't say those horses don't eat well. Here." She turned around, holding out the paring knife and the potato, which still had half its peel on. "You do this better than I do. Get to work."

Malcolm knew when to drop a subject. Easily he stripped the potato of its skin and went on to the next one, the peel paper-thin, unlike the thick one that remained when Jacki undertook the task. "Speaking of dinner, what have you got planned?"

Jacki poured water into the pot and set it on the burner. With a flick of her wrist, a warm, blue flame appeared.

"Yesterday's leftover stew with fresh carrots and potatoes. And don't complain about leftovers." Jacki yanked the pot of stew from the refrigerator. Three other items toppled into the space it left. She closed the door with her shoulder.

Sweetheart jumped out of the way. When the Border collie died, Jacki thought, she'd probably have him put to rest in a refrigerator. "You could always cook a meal, too, you know."

"Roast rabbit?" Malcolm suggested, naming his one specialty.

She sighed. "Never mind."

"Thought so." He let out a dry chuckle. "Besides, I've made my contribution."

"Peeling four small potatoes?" she scoffed, removing them from the table and depositing them in the pot with the carrots. Five little splashes announced their descent.

"Four and a half," he corrected. "And no, I was referring to this." He produced a dusty bottle of amaretto from the pouch that hung off the side of his wheelchair. Amaretto was her favorite liqueur. "Found it when I was cleaning my rifle. Don't know how it got into the gun cabinet."

She looked at the bottle as she stirred the stew. "I do."

"Oh?"

Withdrawing the ladle, Jacki reached for three dinner plates and put them on the table. "Maria liked to, um, lubricate her day along." She said the woman's name fondly. Maria had been their housekeeper until her husband had decided that it was time to move on. No great loss, he had been the second to last ranch hand to leave, but Maria, despite her imbibing from time to time, had been a treasure. "She must have left the bottle behind."

"Her loss, our gain." Malcolm leaned forward and placed the bottle on the table, but it annoyed him, standing on the edge that way. He couldn't reach the center of the table anymore. "Move it to the middle, will you, Jak?"

"Sure." She wiped her hands on the apron and pushed the amber bottle over without missing a beat. "What is it we're celebrating?"

Malcolm moved to the cabinets and took out the silverware. Using his free hand, he propelled himself back to the table. Jacki stepped to one side as she put out three glasses. "Getting through another week. Having Gabriel here." With care he folded the napkins the way his wife had always done. "Take your pick."

Jacki was grateful for the light of hope in her grandfather's eyes. That, she knew, was thanks to Gabriel. "You certainly have taken a shine to him."

Malcolm leaned over to stroke Sweetheart's head. The dog almost sounded as if he was purring in contentment. "Doesn't take long to know if something's good or bad. And I've got a good feeling about him."

Jacki nodded. "So do I."

Malcolm chuckled. "I know."

She gave up.

Dinner was just being put on the table when the front door was opened, then closed. Jacki drew her breath in sharply, aware that her senses suddenly seemed much more finely tuned.

Malcolm let out a satisfied laugh and slapped the arm of his chair. "Knew it."

She hadn't known he was watching her. "Knew what?" she asked self-consciously, dropping her voice. He was going to say something to embarrass her, and she didn't want their conversation to carry.

"You lit up like a Christmas tree as soon as you heard him coming in." His eyes challenged her to deny it.

"And you've been sampling the amaretto."

She turned to face the doorway. She felt her smile freeze ever so slightly as she saw the man who walked in. He was shorter than Gabriel and heavier. And a good deal older.

The man scanned the set table and laughed goodnaturedly. "Well, I sure timed this visit well." He looked hopefully at Jacki.

Jacki forced the smile to stay on her lips as she tried to hide her disappointment. "Why don't you sit down, Frank?"

The heavy-boned, sandy-haired man nodded his thanks. His guileless smile went up to his eyes as they crinkled into tiny slits. "I was hoping you'd say that."

Frank Morgan was their neighbor, and a kindlier man would have been difficult to find. He had helped them as much as he could during their hard times and asked for nothing in exchange except their friendship. And eventually, Jacki thought with increasing despair, her.

She backed away from the table—and bumped into Gabriel. Jacki sucked in her breath as his hands went around her, catching hold of the pot of stew that had nearly flown out of her hands. Jacki let her breath out slowly, but her heart didn't stop hammering. Looking at the pot, she flushed. "Thanks."

He let his hands drop and saw a look of regret flash in her eyes when he released her. "Didn't mean to startle you."

Jacki set the pot on the table. "For such a tall man you move very quietly."

"I come by it naturally." It was one of those vague answers she had come to expect from him.

"New hand, Malcolm?" Frank asked amiably, though appeared to be more interested in Jacki's stew than in any new hand they had hired.

Feeling guilty about her flash of resentment at his intrusion, Jacki took down another dinner plate and grabbed a knife and fork for the unexpected guest. She placed the items before him.

Malcolm did the honors. "Gabriel Goodfellow. Frank Morgan." The old man gestured from one man to the other. Jacki noticed that he gave Gabriel precedence over Frank, even though she knew Malcolm liked the rancher quite a bit. It made her feel warm.

Gabriel nodded a greeting, then looked at Jacki. "If you have company, I can—" He was already backing out the door.

Oh, no, he didn't. Jacki took a firm hold of his arm. "You can sit right down before dinner gets cold. Grandpa even found some amaretto to make you forget that these are leftovers." She moved the bottle toward him.

Gabriel offered her a soft smile. He decided that it might be impolite to tell her that he didn't drink. Instead he took his place at Malcolm's left hand, opposite Jacki. Frank sat down next to her.

Jacki tried to disregard the way Frank looked at her throughout the meal. She did her best to maintain a constant flow of conversation. Any silence, combined with Frank's very obvious, yearning look, would have made her terribly uncomfortable.

It was clear to Gabriel that Frank would have liked to do more than just sit next to Jacki. It was just as clear to him from the way she sat and how she answered Frank's questions that Jacki didn't welcome his attention. The thought gave him a great deal of hope. It always amazed him how hope could grow through cracks of despair with so little to nurture it.

"I hope you don't mind me dropping in like this, Malcolm, but sometimes, even with all the activity going on over at my place, I get a little lonely. A man needs some good conversation," Frank observed, though the look in his eyes told Jacki that he would have accepted silence, if that was all she would offer him.

"You know you're always welcomed here, Frank," she replied.

She didn't want to encourage him, but didn't want to appear unfriendly, either. Frank was a widower, who had made his intentions more than clear to anyone who bothered to look. All she had to do was nod her head and there'd be a ring on her finger. More than that, Los Caballos would immediately become solvent. Frank was well-off and very generous. She knew that he would take good care of all of them.

She could do worse.

She could do better. She raised her eyes and looked at Gabriel, who had apparently chosen that moment to look at her. Their eyes met and held. A sharp thrill vibrated through her. How did he do it? Without words, without any indications, any promises, the man was melting her. She hadn't even kissed him, for heaven's sake. And here he was, making her want things, making her forget everything but him.

"Listen, I do have an excuse for being here," Frank began again, laughing at himself. The man obviously was aware that everyone knew how he felt about Jacki, but it didn't appear to cause him any embarrassment. "I know it's early, but I'd like to invite the two of you to my New Year's Eve party. From where I sit you need a little fun, seeing how—"

Jacki only partially heard him. If she accepted, she didn't want him to misunderstand her reasons. Without thinking, she poured herself a glass of amaretto. It was her second. The stew, perforce a smaller portion than she had anticipated, remained basically untouched on her plate. "All right, Frank. Does your invitation include Gabriel?"

It clearly hadn't, but Frank seemed to recover well. Amused, Malcolm watched the game being played out in front of him. He had noticed that Gabriel's expression throughout hadn't changed in the slightest.

"Sure. Didn't mean to sound as if you were excluded." Frank turned to look at Gabriel. His moonlike face sported a genuine grin. "Everyone's welcome. If you're still here by then."

Gabriel started to reply, but Jacki answered for him. "He'll still be here." She offered the bottle to Frank, who moved his glass toward her for a refill. But when she moved to pass it to Gabriel, he shook his head. He had also declined the liqueur when she had originally offered it. Jacki wondered way. It was a rare cowboy who didn't drink at least a little. It helped while the time away and break the ice when mere words couldn't.

With a contented sigh she poured another half glassful for herself. The thick, amber-colored liquid slid slowly down the small glass of cut crystal, pooling at the bottom. It slid down her throat even more smoothly, teasing her insides. Just as Gabriel did. She smiled at him and set the glass down.

After dinner Malcolm drew Frank aside. "There's some things I've been meaning to ask you about Thunderbolt." He pulled his face into a serious expression.

"Something wrong with the stallion I sold you?" Frank's voice sounded concerned.

"Well, not wrong, maybe," Malcolm conceded. "But he's just not acting like a stallion, if you know what I mean." His look went directly to Gabriel, rather than Frank.

Jacki thought she was going to die, but Gabriel, to her relief, seemed not to notice.

"C'mon, we'll talk about it over coffee and cigars," the old man went on.

Only Jacki caught the hidden smile in his eyes. The old rascal, she thought. Thunderbolt had come from Frank's stable last August. He had sold the stallion to them at a very good price, far lower than the stallion warranted. It had been Frank's way of opening negotiations for Jacki's hand.

It was evident by the look on Frank's face that he would rather have stayed and talked to Jacki, but there was no way to politely refuse Malcolm's offer of coffee and cigars in the den.

Jacki smiled at her grandfather. She knew that other men in his position would have urged her to hurry and make Frank propose outright. The man was kind, generous, and would have been more than willing to help his new family out of a difficult financial situation. Those were all very good reasons to marry a man. And all very dull reasons to marry one, she thought.

"Need help?" Gabriel was at her elbow.

"More than you'll ever know," she murmured, then realized what she'd just said. She felt flustered, not an uncommon sensation around Gabriel these days, she told herself. "Oh, the dishes?"

"If that's what you need help with."

She smiled ruefully. What an odd way to phrase his offer. She gave him the glasses to carry to the sink. "You're a very strange man, Gabriel."

The glasses clinked as he placed them in the sink. "I've been told that."

Jacki covered the last of the stew with plastic wrap. She glanced at Gabriel. "I never quite know if we're talking about the same thing, or if there's some deep, hidden message to be gleaned from your words."

He laughed as he took the pot from her. "You're reading too much into things." He had to move some containers around before he found room in the refrigerator. He let the door close on its own and turned back to Jacki. "Frank seems like a nice man," he observed.

She didn't want to talk about Frank. She didn't want to talk at all. "Nice enough," she murmured.

"He's interested in you." Gabriel cleared the rest of the table.

Jacki took the pile of dishes from him and put them into the sink. She let the water run before adding the detergent. Bubbles began to rise immediately. "Yes, he is."

Gabriel leaned his hip against the counter and tucked his hands under his arms. He watched her expression as he spoke. "I suppose that would be a way to solve your problem."

Was he that uninterested in her? The thought stung, and she found herself speaking harshly. "Maybe for someone else. Not for me. I wouldn't use my body to save the ranch. Maybe that makes me selfish or old-fashioned, but I won't do it." Though the thought had crossed her mind more than once when she was in the depths of despair, the idea that Gabriel entertained the possibility hurt. "I'm not a chattel to be used as barter."

"No," he said softly, "you're not."

No, he wasn't uninterested. He was testing her, she thought, calming down. Jacki drew closer, feeling the need to be near him. "And what am I?"

He wished she wouldn't do that, wouldn't stand there like that, looking so desirable. It made him want her. He did want her. God help him, he wanted her so badly that he ached. He twisted his lips into a half smile. To think he was asking God for help in this. It seemed almost sacrilegious.

She looked at his smoky-blue eyes, and the burning need within her built. The amaretto had created a steady, warm hum through her veins, and she found that she didn't want to act logically. She tilted her head back as her hands touched Gabriel's face. Rising on her toes, she positioned her lips a hairbreadth from his.

And then they weren't even that far.

"You're beautiful," he whispered by way of answer. Gabriel drew her into his arms, wanting to feel her against him as he kissed her, going with instincts that were centuries old. Timeless.

She didn't regret it. She might have been a little startled by the intensity of her own feelings, by the ease with which she kissed a man who was really a mysterious stranger, appearing in her life like an angel. An angel. She felt a giggle build within her. She was kissing an angel. No, there were no regrets, no regrets at all.

He felt her smile curve beneath his lips. It touched and spread within him, feeding a need, setting off alarms. Setting off warnings.

Everything he could imagine was there in her kiss—sweetness, a rare, exotic taste. She was all things to him, a kaleidoscope of womanhood, here in his arms.

Wanting to take, to seize, he forced himself to be gentle.

You're not free to do this, he remembered. She doesn't know.

With effort he drew back. "I'm sorry."

But she didn't want him to retreat. Not yet. Perhaps not at all. "I'm not."

He felt his blood pressure rising again. "It's been a long time since I kissed a woman."

"You haven't forgotten how." It was the liqueur talking, she knew. On her own she couldn't have said that to him.

Gabriel laughed as he slid a hand through her hair and cupped her chin. And then the laughter died as a wave of passion claimed him. He brought his mouth down, this time with more force, more needs burning and slicing away pieces of him. Her mouth was willing, eager, taking him prisoner.

His lips grew warm and heated hers, heated her. She felt as if she were floating. There was an emptiness within her, an emptiness she had not been aware of until this moment, until his kiss had begun to fill it. Jacki moaned and clung to him.

The room was swaying, then everything went black. When she opened her eyes it was still dark. Jacki caught her breath. "What the—?"

Gabriel looked at the dark kitchen. There was no light anywhere. "I think you blew a fuse," he said.

"At the very least," she murmured, sorry for the interruption.

"Where's your fuse box?" Gabriel asked, releasing her.

"Jacki?" she heard her grandfather calling from the den.

"It's just a fuse, Grandpa," she answered, wishing Gabriel were still holding her. It took a moment to regain her ground. "Gabriel's taking care of it." Just as he's taking care of everything else, she added silently.

She took a flashlight from the drawer behind her, and together they found the fuse box on the porch. After a couple of tries, Gabriel discovered the errant fuse and replaced it.

What an odd way to end a kiss that began with thunder and lightning, she thought. She leaned against the railing, unable to draw her eyes from Gabriel.

Gabriel brushed off his hands. "Well, I'd better go. You've got a guest." He nodded toward the house.

"Frank's not a guest. He's a perpetual proposal."

Gabriel thought of what had just happened between them and knew that it was too soon, even though he hadn't been able to help himself. "Still, I'd better go. Thanks for dinner, Jacki."

She nodded silently as she watched him go. She ran her hands along her chilled arms and suddenly felt bereft. Hadn't he felt anything? Had the amaretto made her a fool? No, she had no regrets. She'd wanted to know what it felt like to kiss him, and now she knew. It felt wonderful, heavenly. One taste of honey and she knew that she was going to want more.

Her world was crashing around her, and she was busy falling in love.

Jacki shook her head. Tomorrow, when her head was clear, she was going to give herself a stern talking-to. She looked at the star-filled sky and felt the crispness of winter in the air. With the sun gone, the uncustomary warmth that had accompanied the day had faded quickly. It was going to be a cold night.

He was going to need an extra blanket, she decided. The thought of going to him now buoyed her. Jacki hurried into the back room and fetched one of the old blankets that were stored there. On her way out she passed Frank and her grandfather.

"Where're you going in such a hurry?" Malcolm asked.

She indicated the blanket in her arms. "He's going to get cold."

"Not by my reckoning," Malcolm murmured.

Frank began to rise. "Why don't you let me—?"

"I think I'd like a little more bourbon," Malcolm said, stopping Frank in his tracks. But he couldn't stop Frank sighing as he filled his host's glass and watched Jacki disappear through the door.

Gabriel wasn't in the bunkhouse.

There were no lights on in the old building. For a moment she felt a touch of panic, more than just for herself. If Gabriel suddenly chose to leave as mysteriously as he had shown up, the ranch was going to be in trouble.

Had she scared him off?

She raised her head and looked at the bright moon. Why did she always move so fast when she knew what she wanted? *Restraint* was a foreign word to her—a word she was going to have to become acquainted with. *If* she had a second chance.

And then she heard him. His voice came from the corral behind the stable. It sounded as if he was talking to someone.

Jacki looked back at the house. Frank and her grandfather were still there. Who was Gabriel talking to? Silently she crept along the side of the building, staying within the shadows.

Gabriel, his body highlighted by the bright moon, was leaning against the fence. She could see no one else in the area.

"Well, Boss, we've certainly got our work cut out for us, don't we? It's going to take more than a few mended fences to set this place to rights." He paused, as if listening for an answer, then went on. "But it's my first chance in a long time. I don't want to turn my back on it. On her, really." There was a pause. "Yes, I know. I've got no business with her, not being who and what I am, but still . . ." His voice trailed off.

Jacki stood stock-still. What did he mean, who and what he was? Just *what* was he?

Her head felt dizzy from the liqueur, and she had trouble thinking straight. The word *angel* came back to her. Angel?

Oh, God, she was getting giddy. Maybe it was the amaretto. Maybe it was the stress of holding body and

ACCEPT FOUR BRAND NEW
YOURS

We'd like to send you four free Silhouette novels, worth $9.00, to introduce you to the benefits of the Silhouette Reader Service™. We hope your free books will convince you to subscribe, but that's up to you. Accepting them places you under no obligation to buy anything, but we hope you'll want to continue your membership in the Reader Service.

So unless we hear from you, once a month we'll send you six additional Silhouette Romance™ novels to read and enjoy. If you choose to keep them, you'll pay just $2.25* per volume. And there is *no* charge for delivery. There are *no* hidden extras! You may cancel at any time, for any reason, just by sending us a note or a shipping statement marked "cancel" or by returning any shipment of books to us at our cost. Either way the free books and gifts are yours to keep!

ALSO FREE!
VICTORIAN PICTURE FRAME

This lovely Victorian pewter-finish miniature is perfect for displaying a treasured photograph—and it's yours *absolutely free*—when you accept our no-risk offer.

Perfect for a treasured Photograph

Plus a FREE mystery Gift! follow instructions at right.

*Terms and prices subject to change without notice.
Sales taxes applicable in New York and Iowa.
© 1990 HARLEQUIN ENTERPRISES LIMITED

◆ ◆ ◆ ◆ ◆ ◆ ◆

SILHOUETTE ROMANCE™ NOVELS
FREE!

◆ ◆ ◆ ◆ ◆ ◆

 Silhouette Reader Service™

```
AFFIX
FOUR FREE BOOKS
STICKER HERE
```

YES, send me my four free books and gifts as
explained on the opposite page. I have affixed my
"free books" sticker above and my two "free gift"
stickers below. I understand that accepting these
books and gifts places me under no obligation ever to
buy any books; I may cancel at anytime, for any reason,
and the free books and gifts will be mine to keep!

215 CIS HAYU (U-SIL-R-09/90)

NAME

(PLEASE PRINT)

ADDRESS   APT.

CITY

STATE   ZIP

Offer limited to one per household and not valid to current Silhouette Romance™
subscribers. All orders subject to approval.

```
AFFIX FREE
VICTORIAN
PICTURE
FRAME
STICKER HERE
```

```
AFFIX FREE
MYSTERY GIFT
STICKER HERE
```

◆ ◆ ◆ ◆ ◆ ◆ ◆

WE EVEN PROVIDE FREE POSTAGE!

It costs you *nothing* to send for your free books — we've paid the postage on the attached reply card. And we'll pick up the postage on your shipment of free books and gifts, and also on any subsequent shipments of books, should you choose to become a subscriber. Unlike many book clubs, we charge *nothing* for postage and handling!

soul together for so long. Or maybe it was his kiss that had knocked her sensibilities for a loop.

An angel? What if—?

Hadn't she said he was an answer to a prayer? Hadn't he appeared at the mission, just when she was in the depths of despair, praying for help? What if he was—?

No, it couldn't be. She had kissed him. Angels didn't kiss. Angels didn't come down to earth wearing faded jeans and cowboy hats. They—

How did she know what angels did or didn't do? Or if they were even real?

She remembered the movie she had watched with her grandfather the first night Gabriel had arrived. Every time she turned around, the subject of angels had been raised in some form, staring her in the face. And Gabriel spoke in such enigmatic sentences. What if—? Dear God, what if—?

Her hands felt icy cold as she dropped the blanket to the ground.

Chapter Seven

A sharp intake of breath caught his attention, and Gabriel slowly moved around the side of the stable. He was surprised to see Jacki standing there, a blanket crumpled at her feet. Even allowing for the light of the moon, her face, usually so animated, was pale. She looked frightened.

"Jacki?"

Did she know about him? The question sprang into his mind, making him uneasy. Had she managed to somehow find out?

No, that was absurd. There'd be no way for her to find out about him. But something *had* frightened her. Gabriel gazed around, deliberately scanning the area. Everything appeared the way it should, bathed in the soothing shadows of night. There was nothing to indicate why she should be as startled as she appeared.

"What's the matter?"

He crossed to her quickly and put his hands on her arms. Now she seemed to be about to faint. Jacki felt rigid beneath his hands, so different from the way she had felt against him only a few minutes ago.

Did she know? He couldn't be certain. He only knew that he didn't want her to know about him, not yet, not until he had done more work here first. Then maybe she could accept the truth.

She was being crazy, absolutely crazy, Jacki told herself. Her imagination had gotten ahold of her, that was all. It was just the culmination of all the stress she had endured over the last year. The stress and Gabriel. He wasn't an angel any more than she was. Gabriel felt like a man. He touched her like a man. And could she feel the way she did, could she have these sudden, deep-seated passions for an angel, for heaven's sake? Of course not, she thought almost fiercely.

She forced herself to push aside her groundless suspicions.

"Just a little dazed by the amaretto, I guess," she explained, flashing a nervous grin. "I drink so infrequently that having more than one can have a devastating effect on me. And I guess I did drink them a little too fast."

Jacki looked at her feet and saw the blanket. She felt a little foolish about the way she had reacted. No, she amended, she felt *a lot* foolish.

"I was afraid you might get cold. It seems like we might have an early chill tonight. I just came to give you this blanket." The words didn't flow easily, the way they normally did for her. She was searching for the right thing to say. She wanted to be here, next to him, and yet she felt awkward.

Nerves, Jak, just a case of nerves.

Gabriel bent down and picked up the dark blue blanket. Briskly he brushed it off, scattering a few dead leaves. Tucking the blanket under his arm, he smiled at her. Her words and the look in her eyes didn't go together. He wished he knew why she looked so uneasy. "I don't mind the cold, but thanks."

Could be worse, she thought. He could have said he didn't mind the heat, and then her mind would have gone off in another direction. She might have thought he was a devil. Devils wove magic, too, or spells, or whatever it was that her addled brain was conjuring up, she thought sarcastically. She *was* being a fool. He was no more a devil than he was an angel.

She decided that for the moment it was best to retreat before she made a complete idiot of herself. "I'll see you tomorrow." She took a step back, then turned and hurried away.

Maybe she was feeling awkward because of the kiss, he decided as he watched her disappear. She probably had realized that she had kissed him while "under the influence," and now regretted it.

Gabriel ran his forefinger along his lips. He could still feel it there, and in every part of his body. The sweet, tempting impression of her mouth. She had touched more than his skin when she had kissed him.

Gabriel turned and walked back to the dark bunkhouse. She was unsettled, that was all. There was no reason to believe anything else.

The bunkhouse was both dark and still. He reached for the light switch, then changed his mind. There were times he liked the dark better. Such as now. He didn't want to do anything except lie there and think of her.

Gabriel lay down on his bunk, his fingers laced beneath his head. He watched the tree outside his window cast shadows that advanced and retreated on his wall, its branches teased by the wind. The tension refused to leave his body. He was still uneasy about the way she'd looked at him. He didn't want her to know about him. Not yet. Perhaps not ever.

How could she be so dumb? An angel. He was no more an angel than—than Frank was.

A laugh bubbled in her throat at the comparison. She stopped for a moment and stood on the bottom step of the porch, thinking. She could still see the bunkhouse from here. There were still no lights on. She couldn't stop the shiver that danced through her shoulder blades and then disappeared.

Maybe he didn't care for lights. Nothing wrong with that.

So what had been in that drink he had given her? her mind taunted.

This and that, he had told her.

Mysteries. She came up against nothing but mysteries every time she tried to learn something about him. He didn't seem to want her to know anything. But why? What was he hiding?

Wings.

Jacki laughed at the unbidden thought. Her laugh had a nervous ring to it she couldn't get rid of.

She shook her head. The situation was too muddled to sort out right now. Tomorrow. She'd think it all through tomorrow.

The sound of laughter came from the house. Jacki closed her eyes and pressed her lips together. Frank was still there. It wouldn't do to be rude, even though she wanted to be by herself now. She sighed and went in, comforting herself that she at least had the dishes to hide behind for the time being.

The morning sun burned away her doubts. It had been the amaretto, pure and simple, that had made her have all those impossibly ridiculous ideas about Gabriel.

An angel! She laughed to herself as she braided her hair, then secured the end with a clip. She looked at her reflection in the bathroom mirror. It didn't look like the face of an addle-brained woman, she mused. But she certainly had been last night.

An angel, oh, wow!

She tucked her shirt into the waistband of her jeans as she walked out of the room. Time to get started.

Her mind refused to relinquish the nagging thought that had been born last night in the moonlight. It hung on, the way Sweetheart did to a bone.

Just because Gabriel had arrived to help her for free at at time when everyone else was fleeing, going on to work that paid; just because she found him at the chapel right after she had prayed for a miracle; just because he could cure a headache with something that fizzed when no pill put out by the leading pharmaceutical companies had ever seemed to help her; and just because Sweetheart seemed to follow him around like a docile puppy instead of the ornery, mean-tempered dog that he was, that didn't mean Gabriel was anything more than a flesh-and-blood man.

Did it?

Jacki dragged her hand through her bangs and let them fall. Her arguments were beginning to make a case for the opposition.

Jacki marched into the den, deciding that she was going to put this nonsense out of her mind, once and for all. She had a ranch to run—for however long the obstacles let her.

The den was a cluttered mess, the way it always was after her grandfather spent any time in it. She shook her head and began to hunt for her purse. She knew she had left it in the room somewhere. A purse wasn't much use on a ranch, and she tended to lose track of it. She found it lying beneath a pile of old newspapers that her grandfather had been reading and then had carelessly tossed aside. She scooped up the papers, placed them in a haphazard pile on the coffee table and began to rummage through her purse, looking for her checkbook.

It wasn't there. She struggled with impatience. Her mind seemed to be going in two different directions at once since last night.

The desk drawer. That was where she had seen the checkbook last, she thought. She crossed to the desk and pulled open the middle drawer. Success.

Gabriel loomed in her mind again. Her pulse quickened at the thought of him.

Okay, so who was this "boss" he was talking to last night? And what was this "we" business? If she didn't know any better, if she were simpleminded, she thought, tossing her checkbook into her purse, she would have said that he had been "sent" to her. But people—or other things—weren't "sent." You made your own luck, your own destiny. Your own misfortune.

If that's true, why'd you go down to the mission and pray? she asked herself. There always seemed to be a nagging voice inside her, these days, playing devil's advocate. But the answer to this question at least was simple. Because she'd *needed* to. Some things were ingrained.

Jacki walked out of the den and crossed to the living room. Her grandfather was bent over a checkerboard, intent on beating the wispy-haired, gaunt old man, dressed in a fire-engine-red shirt and rumpled, brown corduroy pants, and seated opposite him. Amos Mac-Cready was her grandfather's oldest friend. The two men had been getting together and arguing over checkers every Wednesday afternoon for as far back as she could remember.

"I'm going to the store for the turkey, Grandpa. When I get back, I'm taking Jasmine out for some exercise." Jasmine was the only one of their five mares that hadn't successfully mated with Thomas McGuire's prize stallion. "She's getting kind of skittish around all those pregnant mares."

Malcolm raised his eyes and gave her a telling look. "I hear single ones usually do."

"I know what you're leading up to, Grandpa, and it won't work." Marriage, always marriage. "Horses don't get married." She kissed him on the top of his head, then winked at his opponent. "Beat the pants off him, Amos."

Amos chuckled as he pulled his shirt sleeves up on rubber-band-thin arms. The sleeves slid back down almost immediately. "I intend to, Jacki. I most certainly fully intend to."

"In your dreams, old man," Malcolm snorted, moving a black checker.

Amos raised gray-tufted brows. "Old man? Old man?? I'm six months younger than you are, Malcolm."

Malcolm shot his best friend a haughty look. It was a familiar game. "Age is in the mind."

Jacki looked out the window. The sun was shining, and the day had the makings of being another warm one. Up and down. The weather couldn't seem to make up its mind, even in the last part of November.

"He's got you there, Amos." She decided to take her jacket with her, just in case. "Most of the time he behaves like someone's twelve-year-old, pesky younger brother." Picking up her jacket and folding it over her arm, Jacki put her tan Stetson on. As she left the room, she moved the strap of her bag higher on her shoulder. It had an annoying habit of slipping off.

"She always was a sassy thing," Malcolm pronounced, watching her go.

"But pretty," Amos countered. "Very pretty."

"Yeah, maybe too pretty for her own good," Malcolm agreed. "I'd feel a lot better if she were married and taken care of."

"Jacki's always been able to take care of herself," Amos pointed out.

"You gonna talk all afternoon or play?" Malcolm demanded.

Jacki laughed quietly to herself, listening to the conversation as she eased the front door shut. When outmaneuvered, her grandfather always attacked. When in doubt, charge forward. The man was a delight when he wasn't driving her crazy.

Sweetheart met her at the bottom step and, for a change, wagged his tail. "Nope, you can't come." She pulled on her gloves. They were of a soft, worn suede, a gift from her grandfather just before his accident. She treasured them. "You know how they feel about dogs in shopping areas, especially you. I know you. You just want to take a bite out of someone new."

Sweetheart turned in the middle of his owner's sentence and darted away as if she had never even come out of the house.

"That's right. Pay attention when I talk." Jacki shaded her eyes and saw that the dog had scented Gabriel, who was emerging from the stable. Like a pied piper, she thought.

Impulse overtook her. "Hey, Gabriel." She stood up in the Jeep and waved at his approaching figure. "Want to take a break and ride into the city?"

Gabriel stopped walking and studied the harness in his hands. He had intended to spend the afternoon mending it. He glanced at the stable. There was time enough later. "I guess this can keep. Sure. Give me a minute."

Jacki nodded and sat back in the Jeep. A feeling of well-being washed over her. She told herself that the reason she felt suddenly so happy was because she liked having company on the ride and because he could do the lifting and the carrying. She also told herself that she was a liar.

She watched him as he approached the Jeep. He moved like a panther, sure of every step. A sleek, well-toned animal. Angels weren't animals, were they? She laughed at herself.

He threw his jacket into the back seat next to hers and was about to step into the passenger's side when she turned to him.

"Do you want to drive?" she offered. In her experience, men preferred handling the wheel. She realized that she was hunting for things to convince herself that he was what he seemed and not what she had so ludicrously thought.

Gabriel shook his head and took his seat. "Thanks, but no. I'm not much good around cars. Horses are more to my liking."

She could understand that, she told herself. It was a rather natural reaction for a man who worked with horses. She started the Jeep. Her silent assurance some-how lacked conviction. "More of a man of the earth," she commented.

"Something like that."

Or the air, she added. Uneasily.

"Don't you want to know where we're going?" Or do you already know? she thought. Her fingers felt damp within her gloves, even as she told herself that she was being silly. Braking, she pulled them off and shoved them into her back pocket.

"Well," Gabriel said slowly, "considering that you've been on the ranch all week, I figured you were going into the city for groceries."

See, all very logical. I swear, Jak, you're getting posi-tively loony.

"More specifically," she said happily, anticipating the following day, "the turkey."

"The turkey?" he asked absently. The wind was pick-ing up, and he tugged his Stetson over his eyes.

She didn't like not seeing his eyes. It made her feel un-easy. *More* uneasy. "Tomorrow's Thanksgiving."

"Oh, that's right." He nodded, remembering. "I guess I forgot."

Of course, an angel would lose track of something so mundane. They didn't celebrate Thanksgiving in heaven.

Stop it, Jak, you're making yourself nuts.

She told herself to keep talking. It was, after all, what she was good at. "Do you miss your family at a time like this? The holidays, I mean."

His family. A faraway smile came to his lips. "It doesn't take holidays to miss someone."

"I'm sorry. I didn't mean to pry." Oh, yes, I did. I'm just sorry I'm not being very good at it, she thought. The look on his face troubled her, although she couldn't quite explain way.

The enigmatic smile gave way to a grin. "I guess I'm not much of a conversationalist."

She couldn't resist his smile or the self-deprecating tone in his voice. "I've had more involved conversations with Sweetheart, but I figure with patience I can get you to come around."

"Maybe." He had a feeling that if anyone could get him to change his ways, this elfin woman with her brand of steel determination could.

Jacki turned on the radio. A golden oldie filled the air. "You are my special angel," the man sang. Jacki switched to another station.

She watched him in the grocery store. She hadn't meant to but couldn't help it. She kept looking for a sign, something to convince her that she was just imagining things and suffering from stress, even as she told herself that she was being ridiculous. Maybe it was her childhood training. She had listened to her grandmother and believed with all her heart when she was told that angels appeared at a time of need.

Or maybe it was that wonderfully sweet movie her grandfather doted on and had made her watch. She could blame this whole thing on Jimmy Stewart.

Or maybe she was plain overworked. But once the seed had taken root, it refused to be weeded out.

Maybe he wasn't an angel, but he certainly seemed out of place in the modern supermarket. A little bewildered and surprised at the quantity of items offered. It was nothing he really did, but the impression was there with her, nonetheless.

"Seems like such a waste of energy and money," he commented, pushing the cart down another aisle for her. He stopped to look at half an aisle full of breakfast cereals.

"Just free enterprise," she assured him, choosing the kind that was her grandfather's favorite.

"I suppose."

"Don't you believe in free enterprise?"

"I don't believe in shrewd competition, if that's what you mean. Just in doing the best job that you can."

"Nothing wrong with that," she answered. Just unusual. Highly unusual, she thought. "Well, we're finished," she announced. "Just push it over there." She indicated a short line and hoped that it would move quickly.

"What's that?" Gabriel pointed to the price scanner at the checkout counter.

Jacki looked at him, surprised that he didn't know what a price scanner was. It made her feel eerie. There had to be a logical explanation for his ignorance. Maybe he just came from a small town in the middle of nowhere, she told herself, trying to steady the uneasiness she felt building within her. After all, price scanners weren't everywhere. Just *practically* everywhere.

"That's a price scanner," she said with false cheerfulness. "It scans electronic coding and tells the computer what you're buying."

"Oh." He looked mildly interested, then turned to study other people in the store around them.

Circumstantial evidence, she told herself as she followed him back to the Jeep. She lifted a bag from the cart and began to deposit it in the back of the car. Gabriel took it from her and found a place for it. Even if he was an angel, which he wasn't, why was she so nervous, so tense? So unhappy?

Because she liked him, that was why. Because she was attracted to him, so much so that everything else that was happening around her was fading back a few yards, getting out of focus. She was still worried about the ranch, still had her hands full, still saw only red ink in the account books, but through it all something was happening, her pulse was quickening, her mind wandering, her fantasies taking off.

And she was having them about an angel.

Maybe she needed help. Serious help.

He touched her shoulder, and she jerked. "What?"

"I said we're done, unless there's something else you want to get while we're in town."

"Yes." My head examined.

"What?"

She shook her head. "Never mind. Let's get this back home. I promised Jasmine a ride."

He thought of the harness that was waiting for him in the stable. And the tack room was sorely in need of a thorough cleaning. But he had a yen to go riding, to feel the wind in his hair and share the experience with a beautiful woman.

She saw him glance at the sky. Was he communing? Getting silent instructions?

Was she losing her mind?

"Want company?" he finally asked.

She would have called it a spontaneous suggestion, if he hadn't paused for so long. Still, she couldn't bring herself to say no. Yes, she wanted company, his company. And her own peace of mind.

"I'd love some. I think you've worked hard enough to merit a day off."

"With pay?"

"Excuse me?" He had lost her. Which, all things considered, wasn't hard.

"Food." He nodded toward the back.

Relief came over her. He was referring to the way he was earning his keep. "That's for tomorrow." She laughed. "But I won't let you starve."

Angels didn't worry about eating, right?

Angels who were trying to pretend to be mortals did.

Jacki turned the key in the ignition. The Jeep purred into life. She didn't have to worry about the second trust deed coming due next month. She was going to be certifiably crazy before then, if she didn't get ahold of herself—and soon.

Jacki rode her horse long and hard, racing Gabriel's big palomino until she felt the wind had whipped her breath away and wiped her mind clean. She had a feeling that he was letting her beat him, that he was holding his powerful horse back, but that didn't matter. Jacki had always liked winning.

When she reached the meadow, she slid off Jasmine, letting the reins drop to the ground. Jasmine was trained to stay. Gabriel joined her in half a gallop.

She raised her face to look at him. He cut such an imposing figure. And cast a deep shadow, she noted happily, hugging the fact to her. "You let me win."

Gabriel swung one leg over the horse and descended in a fluid motion, almost as if he had been born on a horse. "I said I didn't believe in competing. Besides, you look beautiful when you're happy. Like some untamed creature of nature."

She tossed her head back, aware that her eyes were dancing. Her hair had long since come loose from its braid, and she had undone the rest with her fingers. She liked feeling her hair free. "Very poetic."

"No, just observant."

He took a step toward her, and she stayed where she was, her eyes on his lips. She began to feel her blood heating again. "What else do you observe?"

He didn't answer. Instead the meadow suddenly fell silent except for the humming of her own blood. It rang in her ears. He touched her hair gently, his fingers sifting the silken masses slowly. "It's been almost an eternity," he said softly, almost to himself.

An eternity? Oh, God, was he just being vague, or—?

But when he took her into his arms and kissed her, she didn't care whether he was being vague or not. She didn't care what he was being, only that he was kissing her, only that his lips were playing softly, gently, then hungrily on hers. Jacki threaded her arms around his neck, pulling him closer. She felt his hands as they moved up and down her back, stroking her, liquefying her limbs at an alarming rate.

The quick flash of passion had subsided, but not the desire, not the need. He needed her, needed this woman more than he had needed to be free, more than he needed to feel the ground beneath his feet, see the sky above his head. She was quickly becoming his universe. He knew the dangers of that. Yet he couldn't stop.

Although his body demanded otherwise, he kissed her slowly, with the utmost tenderness.

He wanted to touch her, taste her, absorb her into his very being. He deepened the kiss, letting himself go just a little more.

He wasn't kissing her gently anymore. The kiss had fire and light and passion in it, an edgy passion that seemed to consume her. It made her head spin. She held on to his arms, afraid that if she didn't, her legs wouldn't be able to support her.

Her pulse scrambled madly, responding to the increasing pressure of his mouth, to the warmth of his body against hers. The perils of this situation flashed through her mind, then faded into the shadows. If he was what she thought he was, was this a test? Would lightning strike? Would the earth move?

It *was* moving.

Her eyes flew open; she felt the earth tremble beneath her feet. The horses were whinnying in panic as she sprang back, away from Gabriel.

"Earthquake," he said, answering the question in her wild eyes.

He grabbed the reins of both the horses, because she could apparently only stand there, mutely looking at him, then at the sky, her eyes huge with wonder.

The land ceased to shudder and tremble almost before it had even begun. Jacki stood frozen where she was.

"A little one," he commented.

He handed her Jasmine's reins. She looked frightened again, the way she had last night. Why? She was a Californian. Earthquakes came with the territory. And this one was so minor, it was scarcely noticeable.

"Maybe that was just God's way of saying I have no business kissing the owner's granddaughter."

"Maybe," she answered, her voice suddenly hoarse as the meaning behind his words sank in.

He laughed softly, but knew she didn't hear him.

Chapter Eight

There's nothing like a good meal to make a man feel alive," Malcolm commented to Gabriel. He was pleased to have the young man at his table for Thanksgiving. He suspected that it would have been a lonely holiday for Jacki with just the two of them. Having Gabriel there helped take the focus off what might be in store for them in the very near future.

"Or fat." Jacki gave her grandfather's stomach a long glance. She stood up. "Well, all this certainly doesn't look so appetizing anymore, does it?" She laughed, looking at the remnants of the carved turkey and the other plates on the white-covered table. Serious eating had taken place here, she thought with a grin.

She leaned over to pick up her grandfather's dish, and he motioned as if to slap her hand away.

"I'm not finished with the drumstick," he protested. "Worse than Sweetheart," he muttered into his beard.

Jacki narrowed her eyes. She heard Gabriel laugh softly behind her. The sound warmed her. "If you can find any meat left on that, your eyes are sharper than I give you credit for."

The little, round mouth beneath the snowy beard pulled into a grin. His eyes said, "Gotcha," loud and clear. Jacki couldn't help being amused, remembering his declaration that he could see something going on between Gabriel and herself, even when she protested that there wasn't. "That's what I've been trying to tell you, girl."

"Can I have the plate, Grandpa? Sweetheart looks like he's about to go for your throat if he has to wait any longer." She nodded at the dog that stood between them, watching the tug-of-war.

"Here, take it," Malcolm said. "Never let it be said I let anyone starve at my table, even if they were just a dog."

"Sweetheart appreciates your generosity, Grandpa," Jacki said soothingly.

She stooped. As usual, Sweetheart snared his prize before she managed to place it in his dish. "You'd think we never fed him," she murmured.

Slowly she began to clear the rest of the table. Gabriel rose silently to help. "So, are you satisfied with the election results, Grandpa?" she asked, trying to divert his attention from dessert. She might as well have tried to transfer the ocean to the desert, using a teaspoon.

"More or less." He craned his neck to get a better view of the stove. "Pie ready yet?"

Accepting defeat gracefully, Jacki took out three smaller plates and counted out three forks from the drawer below. "Almost." She turned and saw the way Gabriel looked at her grandfather's wheelchair.

"Grandpa insists on being the first down at the voting booth each and every time they hold an election," she explained. "Amos comes by and takes him in his van. We had a special election just before you came to work for us."

"A man's responsibilities don't come to a grinding halt just because he can't walk anymore." The pride behind the words couldn't be missed. Malcolm glared at the oven impatiently. "You're going to burn that pie."

"You're the one who's burning, not the pie," she said evenly, setting the three plates on the table. "I'm just keeping it warm."

Malcolm muttered something unintelligible into his beard. He turned to look at Gabriel, wanting to pull him into the conversation. "A man's gotta vote to keep things on the track, right, Gabriel?"

Gabriel put down the half-empty dish of vegetables on the kitchen counter. "I'm afraid I wouldn't be able to say, sir. Not firsthand."

Malcolm raised his nose to smell the cherry pie that Jacki was lifting out of the oven. He felt his appetite stir as she put the steaming pie on the table directly in front of him. His attention was only partially on the conversation. "Why not? Don't you vote, Gabriel?"

Gabriel felt the need to retreat, but running had never come naturally to him, no more than lying did. He took the carton of milk Jacki handed him and exchanged a glance with her. He saw mild curiosity in her eyes. What would you say, he thought, if you knew the whole truth? Gabriel placed the carton on the table and took his seat again. "No," he said quietly.

Malcolm stared at Gabriel. The pie and his unsatisfied appetite were temporarily forgotten. He drew his small eyes into a squint, as if that would help him understand. For a moment he had trouble reconciling this new information with the image of the man he felt he had taken into his home. "Doesn't your conscience bother you at all for not taking part in the system?"

Jacki saw a rather dry smile play on Gabriel's lips. What was going on behind those eyes? she wondered, almost afraid of the answer. She stood with the knife over the pie, transfixed, waiting for him to say something. Gabriel had all of her attention.

"After taking part in the system, I'm afraid I can't vote."

Malcolm pushed his plate toward Jacki for the first helping. He had already decided that Gabriel's reasons were his own. But that didn't stop his curiosity. "That some kind of a riddle, boy?"

Jacki set Gabriel's piece before him. "Let's drop it, Grandpa. Gabriel has a right to his privacy." With a sigh she took the last slice for herself.

She saw Gabriel give her a smile of thanks.

It wasn't a riddle, she thought. It was an answer. Gabriel meant that by taking part in the system, he had once been a flesh-and-blood man, but now he wasn't anymore. Angels didn't vote. They couldn't vote. There was no reason for them to.

Gabriel glanced toward Jacki as he ate, trying to read her thoughts in her eyes. She had very expressive eyes that said things to him she was unaware of saying. He looked for an indication that she knew his secret now, but there was none. Only confusion. Maybe he'd tell her soon. He knew he wanted to, had even started to once or twice, but the words never came. Though he had no reason to be actually afraid of the truth, suddenly he didn't like the taste of the words in his mouth. Because they might change her mind about him. He straightened slightly.

When she knew him better, perhaps she could accept it, accept him the way he was.

But he had to be sure before he told her.

He absently pushed around the last bit of pie on his plate. He wasn't certain that he'd ever be sure.

Jacki looked at Gabriel's plate, acutely aware of the sudden silence in the room. "Don't you like it?" She wasn't fishing for a compliment so much as looking for a harmless topic to fill the emptiness.

"What? Oh." He looked at the remaining piece on his plate and took the last bite. "It's the best I've ever had."

"She makes a fantastic chocolate cream pie. One bite and you think you've died and gone to heaven," Malcolm testified.

Gabriel laughed. "Well, I—"

Jacki rose to her feet quickly, not wanting to hear what was coming. If he was about to launch into a confession about already having died and gone to heaven, she suddenly didn't want to hear it. She wanted to think of him as Gabriel, her ranch hand, for just a little longer. If that meant she was burying her head in the sand, so be it.

"I think I'll do the dishes now," she announced a bit too loudly. "No second helpings until you digest what's there." Once again she purposely let her eyes slide over her grandfather's rather solid stomach. "Eyes bigger than your stomach, Grandpa—but not by much these days." She patted it lovingly.

She turned to see that Gabriel had gathered his own empty plate as well as hers. She took them from him. For a moment their gazes met and held, each measuring the other. Her heart felt frozen in her chest. She was more afraid than ever that she was right, and she didn't want to be.

Her mouth felt dry. "There's no need for you to help clean up, Gabriel. I can do the dishes. It's Thanksgiving."

"It's Thanksgiving," he echoed, "and I'd like to help. I like feeling useful."

Angels would, she thought.

"Well, while you two debate this, I'm going into the living room to have a smoke and wait until you decide that I can have more dessert at my own table."

"You go into the living room and have a smoke and there'll *be* no more dessert, ever," Jacki told him, putting the stopper into the sink. She didn't even spare him a glance.

Malcolm huffed. "Who's the child here?"

Jacki took out her apron and put the loop over her head. She reached behind her to tie it and felt Gabriel's hands there. She turned slightly, surprised. He offered her a smile as he tied the bow for her. Such a small gesture, such an intimate feeling it created.

"You are," she said, her words unusually subdued, her body keenly aware of Gabriel's nearness, "if you continue to disobey the doctor's orders."

Malcolm struggled to hide the self-satisfied smile that rose to his lips as he observed the two of them together. Won't be long now, he thought happily. He pretended to bristle at the conversation for form's sake. "Hell, the *doctor* is probably kicking back right now, having himself a cigar. Bobby Anderson was always a sniveling, mean-tempered little kid, and just because he's got a degree in medicine doesn't mean he's changed any."

She had to step away from Gabriel to think clearly. Her skin felt warm, very warm. She wondered if a flush was rising to her face. She felt as if it was. Grateful that she hadn't lost her train of thought, she turned her attention to what her grandfather was saying. "Bobby Anderson is a highly respected orthopedic surgeon, and when it comes to mean-tempered, well, you'd be the one to know about that."

Malcolm shook his head as he wheeled himself out of the kitchen. "See what you can do with her, boy," he instructed Gabriel with a shake of his head as he left. But Jacki could have sworn she heard a self-satisfied chuckle right after that.

Gabriel looked in Malcolm's direction. "There isn't anything that can be done about his legs?" He knew about confinement, about the way it could rob one of one's pride, one's self-esteem. And one form of confinement was as much of a hell as another.

"No." She rinsed off a plate and set it on the rack. "Got a miracle cure for that, too?"

Gabriel turned to look at her, puzzled by her tone. "What?"

She shook her head, embarrassed. How had she let that slip out? She didn't want him to confess, to tell her. She knew if he did, he'd be gone. She didn't know how she knew, she just did. "Nothing. Sorry." She turned her face away from him and began to scrub dishes furiously.

But where had that flash of bitterness come from? From her confusion, she realized. Because if he was, if he possibly was, dear God, an angel, then why was he doing this to her? He had to know what she was feeling for him. It had been there in her kiss, in her eyes, probably. Was this a test? Was she failing miserably? Of course she was. A fork dropped into the water and splashed, wetting her cuffs. Mechanically she pulled them back.

What would be the end result of a liaison between a mortal and an angel?

Emptiness.

She stiffened as she felt him touch her hair and brush it aside. Her skin quivered. She was afraid. Wanting more. Wanting him. How could he make such simple little movements feel so overpoweringly intimate?

"Jacki, I want to thank you."

She took a deep breath before she trusted herself to look up. "For what?"

He lifted the dish towel and began to dry a plate. She looked wary. If she didn't know about him, then what was it? What was causing this reaction? "For having me to dinner."

She handed him the next washed plate. "We have you to dinner every night. And to breakfast."

He swirled the dish towel around the plate. "I mean on Thanksgiving."

There was something in his voice that made her stop and study his face. "Why wouldn't we have you here for Thanksgiving?"

He shrugged, taking another plate from the rack. For once he avoided her eyes. "It's usually for families."

"Well, you've joined ours, so to speak," she said lightly, wondering how she could speak when her heart was busy hammering in her throat.

Gabriel put down the towel for a moment. "Don't be too hasty to extend the invitation."

Slowly, ever so slowly, he was luring her in, making her tread near the topic she was so afraid of. "What?"

"I mean, you don't really know me." He looked away.

It was her voice, the nervous plea in it, that made him turn around again. "Then tell me."

"Not yet." He slid his thumb along her cheek, longing to kiss her, longing to make the confession, to be free of the last shackle. Not yet, not yet. The words echoed in his head, pounding in their impression. "There are things I can't tell you about me."

She sighed, bracing her hip against the sink. She licked her lips. "I sort of guessed that." *More than you'd ever know.*

She saw him open his mouth and then shut it again. He wasn't going to tell her, she thought. Relief coursed through her veins like water flowing through a dam that had suddenly collapsed. She didn't want to know, didn't want to hear, because until she heard, until she had the confirmation, there was still hope.

Something giddy bubbled up inside. Hope and angels. Didn't they usually go together? Now she wanted them to travel apart. She wondered if that was blasphemous, especially considering that Christmas was coming up fast.

Would he leave once Christmas was over? Once the decorations were taken down? Would it all be over then? A chill ran over her, blotting out the relief she had just felt.

"Make yourself useful and pick up that towel again, if you're really grateful for dinner," she instructed, struggling to compose herself.

The humor was back in her eyes. He liked the way they seemed to shine. It reminded him of the stars he was so fond of. "Yes, ma'am."

"Where's my dessert?" Malcolm called from the living room.

Grateful for the respite, she cocked her head in the living room's direction. "Are you smoking?"

"Do you smell anything?" Malcolm demanded, acting offended.

"No."

"Does that answer my question?"

"No." She laughed and winked at Gabriel, wiping her hands on the apron. "But I'll bring out another piece of pie for you, anyway."

"About time," Malcolm grumbled. "And bring some for yourselves. I hate to eat alone."

"Ha!" Jacki called back.

She looked over her shoulder at Gabriel. He was smiling at her, obviously reacting to the byplay between her grandfather and herself. It was a smile that curled up her insides, then spread out as if a sunbeam had gotten trapped within her body. It took her prisoner as surely as if he had thrown chains over her.

At that instant Jacki knew she was in love. In love with someone who might be a bona fide, card-carrying angel. Well, no one had ever said she ever followed a well-worn path.

"Gabriel, would you bring the plates, please?" She picked up the pie tin and led the way in.

"Sure thing."

He followed her into the living room. For a little while he'd let himself enjoy the small earthly pleasures that were available, he told himself, content just to be here, sharing the time with this family. And maybe he could stretch it out if he was lucky.

Gabriel walked in and saw Jacki staring at the calendar as if she was mesmerized by it. "What are you doing?" Questions had never been part of his life. He had always been content to wait until the answers came, if any were available. Being around Jacki made questions rise in his mind all the time. She was changing him.

Jacki swung around, startled. She hadn't heard him walking in. Well, why should she? she thought. He didn't have to make noise if he didn't want to. "Gathering my courage up."

He joined her. "For what?"

She couldn't help smiling, despite what she was about to face. "You certainly have learned to ask questions since you've come here."

He helped himself to coffee from the pot that stood on the stove. The burner beneath it was on low, and the blue glow from the flame was almost undetectable. "It's the company I keep."

"Well . . ." She sighed. "You might not be keeping it for long, if my trip into town doesn't go well today."

She looked over and saw that he raised a brow, waiting. She didn't think she had ever met a more patient man—but then, angels were supposed to be patient, weren't they? Why couldn't she find some evidence to point in the other direction? Something that showed her that he most obviously had feet of clay.

No, no, she couldn't afford to get rattled or go off on a tangent today. Today she needed her wits about her. In order to be effective.

"I'm going into town to ask the president of the bank to extend our loan." She nodded at the two place settings and the large dish of scrambled eggs and bacon she had just finished placing on the table. "Help yourself to breakfast. Grandpa'll be out in a few minutes. He had a rather bad night." She sighed. "Thinking about the loan, no doubt." She opened her purse to check the papers there for the fourth time that morning.

But Gabriel didn't sit down. Instead he drained his cup and set it on the counter. "Would you like some company?"

She stopped and looked at him. "To the bank?"

He picked up a piece of bacon. "Yes."

She grinned as she watched him eat. For some reason, the simple act was one of the things she clung to whenever she argued against what she feared was true. Angel or human, though, having him next to her would help put her at ease. She needed self-confidence today. There was no sense in going in to ask for an extension looking as if she knew that the battle had already been lost.

"I'd love it, if you can tear yourself away from the break in the back pasture fence."

He was already putting his Stetson back on his head. Black against black. It made him look even more mysterious. "It's fixed."

"So soon?"

"Yup."

"But there was so much that needed mending." She stared at his face. They had just discovered the long break last week, right after Thanksgiving, when they had gone on one of their few pleasure rides.

"Done."

"Why doesn't that surprise me?" she muttered as she plucked her jacket from the hook next to the door. She paused as he helped her on with it. The momentary contact between them brought with it its customary shiver of excitement. "Maybe you can see what you can do with the bank president."

"Okay."

It almost sounded like a simple confirmation. She didn't know if he was teasing her or being serious. She was almost afraid to find out. No. She *was* afraid to find out. If he was what she suspected, then her problems, monetarily speaking, would be solved. She was sure of that much. Her grandfather would be happy, the ranch would be saved, and she'd wind up being the kind of woman they sang gloomy love songs about around campfires. The legend of Jacki and the angel, or something to that effect. She'd laugh if it wasn't all so painful.

And if he wasn't what she feared he was, if she was just suffering from an overactive imagination stimulated by stress and the power of suggestion, then she might wind up emotionally happy, but lose the ranch. It was truly a no-win situation.

What *was* the secret he was holding back? He had said there was a secret, something he couldn't share with her. If it wasn't that he was an angel, then what was it?

Too many strange things pointed to his being what she didn't want him to be.

Her grandfather entered the kitchen. He looked small and somehow shrunken in his chair this morning. His eyes were tired, and his shoulders sagged a little. She knew he hated what she was about to do, hated the fact that she was the one doing it. He had offered to go himself, but she had very firmly refused. She knew what his temper was like when heated, and she was afraid that an outburst in the bank might be harmful to her grandfather's health. He had enough to endure.

She tried to make herself sound cheerful for his sake. "Grandpa, I'm leaving for the bank now."

"Be sure to wear your cross," Malcolm warned. "Saunders is a blood-sucking vampire," he told Gabriel.

"Grandpa really likes him," she said dryly.

Gabriel only laughed.

"You going with her?" Malcolm asked, seeing the two of them begin to leave together.

"Yes."

He looked a little heartened by the information. "Good. Maybe you can put the fear of God into the man. Nothing else works."

"If anyone can do it, Gabriel can," Jacki said under her breath, then led the way out.

Sweetheart bounded up the steps and placed his front paws on Gabriel's thighs, stretching his head in order to lick his face.

"Gee, you two must have been separated for all of five minutes. What *is* this power you have over animals, Gabriel?" she asked. It wasn't just the dog, it was the horses, as well. She had watched him with the mares in the morning. They responded to his low, gentle tone as if he had always been their master. He had a knack, a gift.

A power.

She shut the thought away, but it kept coming back at her from all angles.

"I come by it naturally."

"I see." The whole problem was, she was beginning to—and she didn't want to.

The trip to the bank seemed shorter than usual. Gabriel asked her several questions about the loan, then turned his questions toward Malcolm's standing in the community. She thought he did it to take her mind off the odious task that lay in front of her. She was grateful to him for that. But they parked in front of the San Juan First National all too soon. She felt her mouth go dry.

"Well, nothing ventured, nothing gained." She stepped out of the Jeep and wiped her hands on the back of her pockets. "Maybe I should have brought Sweetheart with us." She thought of the dog's normal reaction to people. "Nothing like having a snarling dog at your side to make a man come around to your way of thinking."

She took a deep breath and stepped onto the sidewalk. She had to find a way around the obstacles that were in front of them. All they needed was to have the loan extended until spring. Just until spring.

Gabriel opened the glass door for her, and she moved inside. Several people were in the bank, completing their transactions. Business as usual, she thought and then shivered. There was no warmth here.

Without thinking, Jacki reached over and tucked her arm through Gabriel's.

Chapter Nine

Jacki crossed the rust-colored industrial carpet and stopped at the waist-high, oak wall that separated the bank tellers from the rest of the world. Large, framed paintings of the desert and of the Old West, done in warm, earth colors adorned the walls. The decor was meant to generate a friendly atmosphere, to put people at their ease. Jacki knew better.

She looked toward the wall in the right corner and saw the bank president's secretary, a rather plain-looking woman in her thirties. She was squinting at the green glow that was coming from the computer on her desk. Jacki took a deep breath, preparing for the worst, hoping for the best. She could feel Gabriel standing behind her and took comfort in his presence. Man or angel, it was nice having him there with her.

"Hi, Denise," Jacki called to the secretary. The woman in the glasses turned at the sound of Jacki's voice and smiled. Jacki thought she didn't look nearly as plain when she smiled. "Is Mr. Saunders available?"

Gabriel detected an uncertainty in Jacki's voice. He had known her now for three weeks. She was normally so sure of herself in everything she did. He found it an attractive quality in her. This show of vulnerability, though faint, surprised him. It also sounded a chord of protectiveness within him.

Jacki saw Denise smooth back the wisps of hair that were coming loose from her chignon and glance toward the closed door to her left, then bite her lower lip before answering. "He has a ten-thirty appointment with an investment firm, but he can spare a few minutes before then." Her tone of voice hinted that she wasn't quite sure her statement was true. She rose, then hesitated. "Would you like me to tell him you're here?" The look on her face was clearly sympathetic.

Jacki responded to the sympathy, even though she didn't want it. Just because she was in the position of a supplicant didn't mean she had to be rude to Denise, she told herself. This situation wasn't anyone's fault. It just was.

"Please." Jacki turned toward Gabriel. "You don't have to come in with me if you don't want to. It might be a little uncomfortable." She laughed, nervous now. "Mainly for me." But she wanted him in there with her, for courage, for luck, for himself.

Gabriel took off his hat and held it as he looked into her upturned face. "You don't think he's going to give you an extension."

Jacki tried to stifle the overwhelming feeling of defeat that was engulfing her. "No."

"Then why are you here?" The question was straightforward.

She shrugged. Part of her wasn't sure. "I like tilting windmills, I guess, and somehow I can't get over hoping that one morning, that man in there will want to do a good deed for no other reason than just to do one. I—"

"He'll see you now, Jacki." Denise had come up behind her.

Jacki turned to see that Denise was standing to the left of the normally locked swinging door and had opened it. Jacki walked through. "Well, here goes nothing."

Although she sincerely hoped not.

Gabriel followed in her wake and saw the curious, appreciative look that the bank president's secretary gave him. He nodded at her and smiled. The woman took a step back, staring and grinning foolishly.

Leif Saunders rose a fraction of an inch from his seat behind his mahogany desk as Jacki and Gabriel entered the room—purely for formality's sake, she thought. He was tall and thin, and Jacki knew he had been in banking all of his fifty-eight years in one form or another. His father had been the president of the bank before him. He was the kind of person who had a personal interest in each loan that went out and in each foreclosure that came in. He lived and breathed banking, understanding figures and spreadsheets far better than he understood people, she reflected wryly.

Jacki was aware that Saunders's sharp, crystal-gray eyes had assessed her and the man behind her in less than half a minute. She firmly believed that the old adage Time Is Money was stitched across his undershirt and quite possibly tattooed on his chest.

With a wide hand that would have been better suited to manual labor, Jacki noted, Saunders gestured to the two vacant chairs before his gleaming desk. "Well,

Jaclyn, this is a surprise." There was no life in his smile. "Have you come to pay off the loan early?"

She fought the urge to look down and met Saunders's eyes head-on. They both knew he didn't believe his own question. "No, I've come to ask for an extension." She was surprised at how calm she sounded, considering the state of her insides.

The perfectly styled gray hair never moved as the man slowly shook his head. "Jaclyn, we've been all through this before."

Jacki gripped the arms of the French provincial chair to keep her hands from gripping Saunders's throat. "Yes, I know, but I thought that perhaps—"

"This is not personal," he emphasized, his voice a shade softer, no doubt for effect, not because of any feelings on his part.

No, it wasn't personal, she thought. If it was, the man would have made allowances. Allowances could *always* be made. But Saunders was all bank. There was nothing wrong with that, but there was nothing right with it, either. Jacki could have killed for a little kindness right about now.

"I realize that, but I was hoping that—" she began again, but got no further.

"I cannot run the bank on hope, Jaclyn. I'm sure you appreciate that fact. We've been as generous as we possibly could."

No, she wanted to say, you could still be more generous. You could roll the ranch's note over until the spring, or at least for another month or so. No one would be hurt if you did that. Your precious ledgers could support that sort of action.

But she didn't say anything of the kind. Saunders did not have a nodding acquaintance with acts of human kindness or goodwill. His father did, she knew, but the old man had retired from the bank just when her grandfather had had his accident. It seemed as if everything on earth was against them.

"Four of our mares have foals due in the spring. I've already spoken to prospective buyers. Once we sell the foals, we can make the ranch work again. We've got a good start." Her voice began to rise. "Don't make it into an end."

He drew together a neat pile of paper, making sure that the corners were completely lined up. He made her think of Caleb. "I have nothing to do with it."

"You have everything to do with it." She felt Gabriel cover her hand with his own. Looking down, she saw that her knuckles had gone white.

"There are rules and regulations, Jaclyn." Saunders paused, scrutinizing her. "What if the foals don't make it?"

"They will," she insisted.

If possible, his voice was even calmer than before. "I'm not a gambler, Jaclyn, only a simple banker, and I'm afraid the terms of the loan are quite clear. Now, if you'll excuse me..." He nodded curtly at Gabriel and then at Jacki, clearly dismissing them. "I'm expecting someone shortly." He didn't bother to rise. Instead he went back to his work, ignoring them totally.

Jacki felt her heart sink again. She was hardly conscious of getting up and out of the chair. She felt Gabriel's arm on hers as he guided her toward the door. She wasn't even sure why she had come, she realized. Perhaps it was the hope she had built up, watching things going so well in the last three weeks. Perhaps it was because Gabriel was here with her now. Somehow she'd thought that it would make the difference, that it would turn things around for them.

She looked at him, feeling foolish as they stepped into the street. "You're right. I shouldn't have even tried."

"No," he said with quiet deliberation, "I never said that. I just asked why." He looked down, then again at her. His grin was sheepish. "Looks like I forgot my hat." He turned around and walked back into the bank. Jacki followed him in.

Several of the tellers looked at them curiously. It was a small bank, and everyone was acquainted with the dealings that went on.

Gabriel held up his hand to stop Jacki. "No. Why don't you stay right here? It'll only take me a moment. And I don't think you want to see Saunders again so soon."

She was grateful for his understanding. "No, not really."

She watched as he signaled to Denise to open the side gate for him. Charms people just like he does animals, she mused absently, fighting back the feeling of emptiness that was threatening to overpower her. Denise offered her a chair, but she declined. "He'll be back in a second. Forgot his hat," she murmured, leaning against the railing.

She had been fooling herself these past few weeks, letting her imagination get the better of her about the ranch, about Gabriel. There were no miracles with her name on it, no reprieves coming from the governor at the eleventh hour. The ranch would be gone before Christmas and—

"Jaclyn?"

Jacki turned sharply and looked up as she heard Saunders say her name. The man was standing outside his office, looking oddly subdued. There seemed nothing pompous about him now. Gabriel, Stetson in hand, was standing unobtrusively to one side.

Jacki drew her attention back to Saunders. "Yes?"

He looked definitely uncomfortable. "Would you mind stepping back into my office for a moment?"

She looked at him suspiciously as Denise held the door open for her. "No, I don't mind."

Was he going to ask for the money now? Had he decided to play the hard-hearted banker to the hilt? No, he couldn't ask for the money early, even if he wanted to. She still had a little time left.

She heard the office door close and waited until Saunders walked around her to his desk. He leaned his hand on it, as if he needed to touch base with something solid.

"I, um, have been giving your little problem more thought."

In the last three minutes? What was he up to? She glanced at Gabriel. His eyes seemed to encourage her. Her agitation began to abate. "Yes?"

Saunders appeared too tense—or too uncomfortable—to sit down. Jacki couldn't decide which. He smiled, and once again there was no feeling there. But this time it didn't matter. All that mattered was the words she was hearing.

"And I see no reason why, say, in the spirit of the season, we can't extend the loan until at least the second week—" He glanced toward Gabriel and amended, "No, the end of January."

"The end of January?" she echoed in disbelief. Was she dreaming? Was he really going to—?

She looked at Gabriel. For a moment her heart stopped, then thudded on. He was smiling at her. It was a very gentle, inscrutable smile. Nerve endings rose inside her. Peace was gone. In its place were joy, agitation and a host of other sensations, all mixed together. They had bought themselves some time! It was nothing short of a miracle—

A miracle. Her throat went dry.

"That would be wonderful," Jacki said slowly, forcing herself to look at Saunders, when all she wanted to do was stare at Gabriel.

Denise appeared in the doorway. "Mr. Saunders, Mr. Wainwright from the foundation is here," she said softly, clearly afraid to disturb the president of the bank. Saunders's temper was a matter of record with his employees.

But this time there was no annoyance at being interrupted. On the contrary, Saunders received the news like a reprieve. "Yes, yes, well—"

"We'll be going now, Mr. Saunders," Jacki said quickly, "and thank you. Thank you." She remembered to shake his hand, but barely felt his flesh against hers. All she could think of was that they had gained almost another two months' reprieve. That, and the fact that Gabriel had somehow engineered it. She looked at him as they left the office. "Thank you," she repeated.

He looked at her face. His expression was innocent, but she had learned to see past that. "I just went in to get my hat."

"Of course."

Her mind was in a daze. She was right. She *had* to be right. There was no other way that Saunders would have changed his mind. Short of being threatened with murder—and in that case, he'd be shouting for the police—there was no way that man would have given her an extension without divine intervention.

Or angelic intervention.

She eyed Gabriel in silence, feeling the entire spectrum of emotions course through her veins. She was euphoric that the extension had been given. Wars had been won in two months' time. Who knew what was around the bend and what she could do, especially with an immortal champion at her side? But by the same token, if Gabriel was what he seemed to be, and she was having fewer and fewer doubts that he was, then what was she going to do?

Damn it, she was in love with an angel. She glanced at the sky, which was darkening unexpectedly. Was that blasphemous? Thinking damn and angel in the same sentence? Well, she didn't care, she thought irritably. It was a damnable situation to be in.

"Something wrong?" Gabriel asked as they got back into the Jeep.

"What could be wrong?" She started up the car and threw it into Reverse. Glancing over her shoulder, she had a sudden urge to hit something, but controlled it. "We've just been standing before the wolf, and instead of him devouring us, he's suddenly agreed to put his appetite on hold and let us have another two months of life." She righted the wheel and sped away, stepping hard on the gas. Tires squealed.

"Let your foot up on the gas." He reached over and put one hand over hers on the steering wheel.

She looked at him belligerently and was immediately ashamed of her action. "I thought you didn't know how to drive."

"I didn't say I didn't know how. I just said I prefer horses. Now slow down." Grudgingly she did. He let go of the wheel. "By your rather rambling comment, I gather that you're not very happy."

"Not happy? I'm ecstatic." Angrily she brushed away a sudden tear that appeared.

"Tears of joy?"

"Something like that."

They drove in silence except for the ominous rumblings overhead. She tried putting on the radio. The deejay announced that the next record he was going to play was "Devil or Angel." Jacki shut off the radio.

They were about five miles away from the ranch when the Jeep backfired, sent off a few grinding noises and then came to a jolting halt. Stunned, Jacki tried the ignition again. The car refused to start.

"Wonderful," she muttered.

She slid out, and Gabriel came around from the other side. They met at the hood. She stared into the engine, but there was nothing really to see. It was one great big mystery to her. To make matters worse, the sun had completely disappeared and it was suddenly growing dark. It looked as if a storm was coming their way about two months ahead of the normal rainy season.

It seemed to her that ever since Gabriel had arrived, they were having a spate of very unusual weather.

She looked at him hopefully. "Can you fix it?" she asked.

Gabriel shook his head. "I really don't know the first thing about engines."

"That's right." She shut the hood with a bang. "I forgot. They were after your time."

"What?"

She waved away her comment. "Just mumbling. Look, I'm sorry I snapped at you before. It's just that my emotions are all in such a turmoil—"

"No need to explain."

No, you know, anyway, right, she thought, but forced a smile to her lips. He had helped her, she reminded herself. That was what she'd wanted, what she had prayed for. How was he to know that she'd fall in love with him? Angels had no experience with earthly love.

She glanced at the sky. "Well, we can't stay here. The Jeep doesn't have a top, and it looks like rain. We'll get soaked."

Gabriel gazed around them. They were in the open, in a large field. "Didn't we pass a shack on the way here?"

She looked at him dumbly for a second, trying to remember. And then it came to her. "That's right. The old Willows place. It's nothing more than a run-down shack. I think a caretaker once lived in it. It's been there forever. When I was a kid, I thought it was haunted. At least that's what Caleb told me. Caleb and I played there a couple of times. Maybe the noises I heard were Caleb." She took his hand. "C'mon, it's that way." She pointed to the north. A large drop hit her in the face. "We'll never make it in time, but let's make a run for it, anyway."

They made it to the shack, just before sheets of rain began to fall from the sky. She stood panting on the rickety porch, watching the fierce waves of rain beat against the ground.

"Doesn't look like it'll let up soon."

She thought of her grandfather. Today was Wednesday, and that meant Amos was there with him. But he'd still be worried about her. "No." She shook her head. "It doesn't."

Gabriel pushed the front door open. It creaked as it moved slowly, held in place by only one hinge. "We might have to spend the night."

She turned and looked inside the dark, rotting shack. Despite herself, despite the fact that she was much older than she had been the last time she was here and no longer believed in ghosts, she shivered. "In there?"

She made him think of a little girl. He knew she wouldn't like the comparison, but he thought it endearing. "It would be a little warmer in the shack than out here. And drier."

She could hear several places where the rain was coming in through the tattered roof. "I wouldn't make any bets on that."

He laughed and took her hand, and she felt the same charge of energy she always did. Probably happened every time an angel touched you, she thought, trying to remain detached. Somehow nothing about this day seemed very real anymore.

"C'mon," he promised, "you'll be safe in there with me."

I'd be safe anywhere with an angel at my side, she thought, but hesitated for a moment, before she finally followed him in.

"Old habits die hard," she said when he looked quizzical at her reticence.

The smell of rotting wood engulfed her senses as soon as they stepped inside. It was dark in the shack, and she had trouble discerning shapes. She could, however, hear noises. The sounds of tiny, scurrying feet.

"Mice," he whispered against her ear, feeling her tense beside him.

Angel or not, he was making all sorts of things happen to her, just by breathing against her skin. Things couldn't go on this way, she told herself. Jacki pulled back, needing to be in the open. She felt as if the walls were closing in on her from all sides. Gabriel held her hand fast as she tried to pull free and head for the door.

"What's the matter?"

"The mice were here first. Squatters' rights," she elaborated, raising her voice to be heard over the sound of the falling rain.

Her hand was icy in his. Could she actually be afraid here in the dark? Jacki? He couldn't make himself believe that. Yet what other explanation was there?

"Jacki, there are no ghosts, no things that go bump in the night."

She ran her hand nervously through her wet hair. Her hat hung by its drawstring around her neck, blown back by the wind. "You'd be the authority there."

There were times he didn't understand her. "Sometimes you say the strangest things."

"Sometimes I think the strangest things." Like what it would be like to make love to an angel.

The thought almost made her laugh out loud. She was still a virgin. There had never been anyone in her life who'd tempted her enough to make her want to give such an intimate part of herself as a gift. Wouldn't it be incredibly odd to have an angel be the first one to make love with her? Would she still be a virgin after that? Or would she be in some halfway house in between? After all, it wouldn't be as if she had really made love with a man, not really.

Could angels make love? Hadn't she read somewhere as a child that they were genderless? She couldn't remember.

She glanced at Gabriel, who was still holding her hand and looking at her very oddly. His profile was silhouetted in the light that was struggling in through the dirty windows. He looked rugged and totally masculine.

Maybe he hadn't read the same book she had on angels. Maybe he didn't know he was supposed to be genderless.

And maybe she was going crazy.

He heard her sharp intake of breath. She *was* frightened. "Your hand is like ice." He rubbed it between his own.

She tried to pull back. "Don't do that."

"Why?"

"Because you're making it warm." Because you're making me warm, and we both know that's not right. A two-month extension on the loan, and she'd never been more miserable in her life.

He wondered if perhaps she were overworked. "That was the idea."

She shook her head and withdrew her hand. Restless, she began to pace around the shack. Old, broken glass crunched under her boot. "Not a good one."

"You want to be cold?" He looked around the shack and saw a fireplace at the far end, opposite the bed.

She ran her hands up and down her arms, wishing the rain would end. "It's a little more complicated than that."

Gabriel knelt by the fireplace and leaned into it. He could see a gleam of light coming in from overhead. Good. That meant that the chimney was clear.

He sat back on his heels and looked in her direction. "Does this complication disallow having a fire in the fireplace?"

"No." She crossed to him. She didn't like standing alone in the dark. "If you can get it to work."

"Fireplaces I have no problem with. It's machinery that's always given me trouble." He rose and looked again around the room. Amid the cobwebs and the dirt he saw several broken chairs, surrounding a rickety table. Scraps of an old, yellowed newspaper lay on top of it. "This'll do fine." Moving to the nearest chair, he broke a piece off, using his leg as leverage.

Jacki watched as the newspaper found its way into the fireplace followed one by one, by the legs of the chair. Gabriel rooted through his pockets until he found a book of matches.

"I didn't know you smoked." She had almost said, "I didn't know angels smoked," but had stopped herself just in time.

"I don't. These are your grandfather's. I lit his pipe for him yesterday." He grinned at her sheepishly. "He didn't want you to know." He struck a match and dropped it on top of the paper, hoping that would do the trick. There were no more newspapers to help get the fire going.

"He's like a kid, always trying to get away with something. I hate anything that might shorten his life by a day—"

"Sometimes," Gabriel told her as he rose to his feet, satisfied with the fire's progress, "it's not the quantity of life as much as the quality." He moved closer to her, drawn there by things he couldn't name.

Her hair, nearly dry now, looked warm, inviting in the glow of the firelight. He wanted to touch it, to caress her. The longings were back, hitting him hard, making him remember another time and place when he'd been free to be himself, able to offer himself without hesitation. He reached out and touched a curl that lay against her cheek.

Looking into her eyes, he ran the backs of two of his fingers along the path of the wayward strand.

She felt desire take a bite out of her, demanding tribute, demanding a place.

He saw something stir in her eyes. Fear? Desire? He didn't know, but couldn't hold himself back any longer. Just a touch, just a taste, that was all he wanted. He could be satisfied with that. So little to ask for. So very little, but he could be content. "We really shouldn't be here like this," he said softly.

"I know." She didn't move when he slipped his arms around her waist and gently drew her to him.

"And you shouldn't be in my arms like this."

She placed her hands on his forearms. Solid. He felt solid. Like a man. And if he wasn't, she'd pay a price for it. But not now, later, much later.

"I know."

Her voice feathered along his senses, and a fire took hold that blazed much brighter than the one that burned behind them. "And I shouldn't be kissing you."

Jacki rose on her toes. "We'll talk about it later," she whispered, her mouth a breath away from his.

His lips covered hers as he pressed his body against her, drinking in the sweetness so deeply that his head spun. Even better than before, he thought, although that had been exquisite. Like wine, drugging the senses, yet making them alert, making them aware of every nuance.

The fire sparked to life instantly. There was no prelude, no warning. It burst upon him fully grown. His kiss turned desperate, desperate for what he knew was there. He ran headlong into the excitement, the passion that was waiting for him.

He would have to tell her soon, he thought, slanting his mouth across hers. There was no putting it off for too much longer, but until she knew, until he told her, he could pretend that it wouldn't change anything between them, that it didn't matter—that he was an ordinary man, free to love and to have passions.

He ran his hand over her hair, absorbing everything about her. She was like fresh, spring rain after an endless drought and he drank deeply, savoring every drop, yearning for more.

She felt his lips as they roamed her face, tasting, touching, teasing her cheeks, her lids, her forehead, her lashes, her nose. Everywhere he touched, she felt herself melting. She knew she should be issuing a disclaimer, saying that she wasn't that kind of a girl. But she was. This time she was.

She wanted to make love with him. Now.

She wanted him, and nothing else mattered. It was as if the heavens had arranged this, arranged the rain, just for this moment. It didn't matter who or what he was, that the floor was dirty, or that regret would be ready and waiting for her in the morning.

Only this moment counted.

She heard him moan as she pressed closer to him. The sound fed the yearning within her and made her want more.

The white light flashed through the cabin a moment before the hard, rolling peal of thunder crashed about them. Jacki jumped back, her heart hammering in her throat, her eyes wide.

"What was that?" she cried.

Gabriel took her back into his arms, trying to calm her. He had seen horses frightened like this in a storm, but never a person. "It's thunder, Jacki, only thunder." He smiled, trying to soothe her. "It seems that every time I kiss you, the forces of nature try to interrupt."

"Yeah." She swallowed hard, then backed away from him, drawing a deep breath. "I think we should go home."

"It's still raining," he pointed out. She was frightened again. Was it because she knew that they were teetering on the edge? That within another moment he would have thrown reason to the wind and made love to her, slowly, worshipfully? Was that why she looked so afraid? The reason still eluded him.

She stepped to a window. A warning. She had been issued a warning. A very loud one.

"It's not raining that hard anymore," she said, a bit too brightly. "Besides, I don't like the idea of my grandfather being alone and worrying about us."

"Isn't Amos with him?"

He remembered everything. "Yes, but I'd still rather be there with him."

He understood. "And," he reminded her, replacing her hat on her head and adjusting the drawstring, "he hasn't heard the good news."

"News?" she echoed dumbly. He was an angel. There was no other explanation of why fuses blew and the earth moved and thunder crashed when she kissed him. What was she going to do? What in heaven's name was she going to do? Die of anguish?

"About the loan being extended."

Oh, yes. Another of his miracles, she thought, pushing the trace of bitterness away. "That's right, he doesn't know yet. It'll make him very happy."

She forced a smile to her lips.

But it never reached her eyes. Gabriel noticed and wondered why.

Chapter Ten

Any satisfaction that Jacki might have felt as a result of the morning's success at the bank was completely negated by the sight that greeted her as Gabriel and she approached the ranch. Although the house, stable and bunkhouse remained intact, lightning had struck the barn and reduced part of it to kindling.

"Omigod, Grandpa!" Jacki ran into the house, half-formed, frightening thoughts racing through her mind. "Grandpa?"

Amos rose from the sofa and crossed toward them as Malcolm maneuvered his wheelchair to face Jacki and Gabriel. Malcolm tried to hide his feelings, but the look of concern on his face was evident.

"Right here. Lord, missy, you look like something the cat wouldn't drag in."

"Thanks, I was worried about you, too." She reached over and hugged him hard, relieved to find that he was all right. Neither seemed to care that she was soaking wet. "The barn—" she began.

Amos shook his head. "Sorry, Jacki, there wasn't anything I could do."

"No, of course not." She took a deep breath. "The horses?"

"In better condition than you are, according to Amos," Malcolm told her.

"I never compared them to Jacki," Amos protested.

Jacki slowly let out the breath she was holding. She pushed the wet hair back from her face and smiled her gratitude at her grandfather's friend. "Thanks for staying here with him."

"Don't thank him." Malcolm bristled. "The man's afraid of storms. He wouldn't have left until it blew over, anyway. Right, Amos?"

"Whatever you say, Mal."

She moved to the window. The barn stared back at her, a dark apparition of what had been. God, it might have been the stable—or the house. Suddenly she felt grateful, very grateful.

She sensed Gabriel behind her and reached out her hand. He took it and linked his fingers with hers.

"It might have been a lot worse," he said.

"Yes, I know." She wondered if the ranch had remained protected because of him, even though he had been out with her.

"How come the two of you were so late getting back?" Malcolm asked.

Jacki turned from the window. "The Jeep broke down about five miles from here."

Amos stopped as he struggled into his jacket. "Any idea what's wrong?" he asked.

She shrugged. "It just died."

"Where is it, on the main road?" Jacki nodded in re-ply. "I'll see what I can do about it in the morning," Amos promised.

"See that you don't blow it up," Malcolm warned.

"Lovable old coot, isn't he?" Amos chuckled, pull-ing on his hat. "Well, see you all in the morning."

"Thanks again for everything, Amos," Jacki said, walking him to the door.

"My pleasure, Jak." When he winked, Jacki could have sworn that Amos MacCready looked thirty-five years younger and was on the prowl.

It wasn't until half an hour later, when Jacki was sit-ting beside Malcolm, sipping hot chocolate and wearing a fresh change of clothing, that she remembered to tell him about the loan's extension.

Amos was as good as his word. He returned before noon the next day and had Jacki's Jeep humming before dark. He refused any money, but did stay for supper, saying that perhaps Jacki would keep him in mind when it came time to sell the foals. He celebrated his friends' good fortune over getting an extension from the bank and went on his way.

"He's a nice old man," Jacki commented, clearing the table.

"Yeah, if you like that sort," Malcolm snorted. But he was grinning.

"Well," Jacki began, "you two go ahead and have coffee, I've got bills to juggle and accounts to play with."

With the best of intentions Jacki sequestered herself in the den.

An hour passed. The large, worn ledger lay open on top of the scarred desk. She sat, passing a pen from one hand to the other, oblivious to the figures before her. Her mind wasn't on her work. It was on the man in her living room, the man who was allowing her grandfather to entertain him. The man who seemed to be putting everything in her life in such perfect order. Everything *except* for her life. That was in complete turmoil.

"Figures, Jak, just concentrate on the figures." Deliberately she thumbed through a stack of bills that were neatly piled up on the corner of the blotter. All overdue, some more than others.

With the extension from the bank there was a temporary stay of execution. They had sufficient funds now to pay the feed bill and the vet. Those were the immediate accounts to face, now that the bank note had temporarily faded into the background.

But for how long? She let the bills fall through her fingers and land haphazardly on her desk. For a moment she stared at them.

It was almost as if she were twirling the cylinder on a gun barrel loaded with only one bullet. Eventually the bullet would click into place. It was only a matter of time. What did it matter that she kept the ranch running for thirty-nine more days or stopped right here, right now?

Because, a little, unstoppable voice within her said, tomorrow might bring something wonderful, something unimaginable, some bright knight to save her, the U.S. cavalry riding to the rescue.

"Michael the Archangel. Or, in this case, Gabriel," she muttered to the dog, who stood scratching at the door. She pushed her chair away from the desk. One of the wheels went the wrong way and refused to budge until she applied more pressure. It figured. Everything seemed to be giving her a hard time these days, especially her common sense.

"You want to get out, don't you? Don't care so much for my company now that he's here, do you?" She crossed to the door, and the dog fairly danced from one foot to another. "I always knew you were fickle. There." She gestured out the door. "Go. Enjoy."

Sweetheart seemed to take no notice of her as he dashed off to the living room. Jacki leaned against the doorjamb, her hand on the doorknob, ready to close it. She couldn't make herself do it.

Laughter. The sound of laughter floated from the living room. He was making her grandfather laugh. She stretched the muscles in her shoulders and sighed. God, life had changed since he had come here. Gabriel was good for everyone and everything, the ranch, her grandfather, the dog's disposition.

And her?

Was he good for her? she mused, feeling a bittersweet pang pass through her. He was, if he was merely a mortal man with wing-tipped boots rather than wings.

She laughed then, thinking how absurd it would all sound to someone else, if she voiced her feelings. And yet there was so much evidence to the contrary, so much she couldn't explain away except by accepting the notion that Gabriel was really a celestial being sent to help her.

"Why?" she murmured to herself, still keeping the door open.

There had never been any real answers in religion for her, only questions. Questions and blind faith. Nothing clear-cut. God was supposed to provide for the lilies of the field, wasn't He? And the sparrow, right? They weren't particularly good or bad, they just were. Another mystery of faith. Maybe that was why Gabriel was here. To do a good deed just because. Another mystery of faith.

She held her head. If she continued with this, she was going to wind up with one of her headaches. That shouldn't bother her, she thought sarcastically. Gabriel could always cure it with that fizzing potion of his.

Jacki took a step back to the desk and then stopped. Whom was she kidding? Anything she did now, she would only have to redo later. Her mind wasn't functioning clearly enough to work on the books tonight. She needed a break, she decided.

The laughter drew her out. If she stayed inside the den, throwing tidy little numbers around and thinking, she'd go crazy. If she was going to do that, she'd rather do it in the open, amid family and—friends. The term brought a smile to her lips.

He saw her smiling as she entered the room. It was the smile that haunted his dreams at night and took away the boredom as he worked for hours by himself. It was the way he always thought of her, a composite of beauty, innocence and sunbeams.

Jacki nodded her head absently at the two men and perched a little self-consciously on the edge of the sofa near her grandfather. She folded her hands in her lap, her fingers laced tightly together.

Malcolm looked from Jacki to Gabriel. He wasn't wrong. He felt the tension, felt the electricity hum. There was a match here. He wondered how long it would take them to figure it out for themselves. He wasn't above prodding, but the final move, the final decision was theirs, that he knew. Anything else wouldn't stick.

Jacki noticed the family album open on the coffee table. "Is that why you two are laughing?"

She pointed to the opened page. There were several shots of her as a gangly child, standing next to her brother. He hadn't smiled, not even then. Smiling was a waste of energy. Not a single wasted movement could be credited to Caleb. Economy, always economy, until he had gotten to where he wanted to be. Top of the heap. Problem was, Jacki thought, he saw that Los Caballos was part of his heap, as well.

Malcolm squinted at the photograph. His glasses lay on the table next to the album, but he refused to reach for them. Cantankerous pride, Jacki thought, but said nothing. He had a right to his way of doing things.

"That?" Malcolm tapped the page, taking care not to touch a photograph directly, just in case it wasn't the one she was referring to. "I was just telling Gabriel about Caleb. The time I got him out of trouble with the state troopers. Remember?" He chuckled again, reliving the memory and the look on Caleb's face.

She remembered. If she lived forever, she didn't think she'd ever be able to understand what had made Caleb the way he was. He was so different from her. The inter-workings of a family, the interdependence, meant nothing to him. Caleb had hated being in debt to his grandfather. He had always taken great pride in handling things for himself. But the law tended not to believe contemptuous eighteen-year-olds, even when they spoke the truth. Not if the proper politeness wasn't there. And Caleb always managed to irritate people. It was thanks to his grandfather's intervention that her twin brother hadn't been forced to spend more than one night in jail next to drunk drivers, petty thieves and worse, because of a scam he had gotten himself mixed up in quite by accident. It had involved two of his craftier acquaintances—Caleb never had friends, she remembered—and they had made him the fall guy. Malcolm had swiftly gotten to the bottom of it, and Caleb had been released.

Caleb had left for college shortly after that. The words "Thank you" had never been uttered to the man who'd made his education possible.

She wanted to say thank-you now to her grandfather, because he had cared—for all the times he had cared. She leaned over and squeezed his hand.

Malcolm looked at her quizzically. "Hey, what's that for, missy?"

"Nothing."

"Okay." He looked toward Gabriel and resumed his story. "Mad as a wet rooster he was. For a bit I thought of leaving him right where he was, but Jak here pleaded. She's always had a soft spot in her heart for loners and misfits."

Do you, Jacki? Gabriel thought as he looked at her. Do you really?

Why was he looking at her that way, she wondered, as if he were searching for an answer? But what was the question? Probably how she felt about loving an angel. The answer was, she felt awful, but there wasn't a thing she could do about changing it. She did love him.

Malcolm looked at the open page on the coffee table. "Caleb was both, a loner and a misfit. But he was also a hard worker, I'll give him that. A hard worker and damn lucky."

"Too bad he doesn't like sharing his luck with family," Jacki said with a sigh. Restless, she thought of the bills in the next room and ran a hand through her hair. "A handy check from him could pay off the loan for us and keep us afloat until after the foals are born. After that I could repay my kindhearted brother with interest, even though technically—" she gave her grandfather a look "—he owes you that money because you put him through college."

"I didn't expect anything for that," Malcolm told her, dismissing the subject.

"And you certainly didn't get it, did you?"

It was hard to miss the bitterness in Jacki's voice. "You've asked him." It wasn't a question on Gabriel's part so much as an assumption. Sweetheart positioned himself beneath Gabriel's outstretched hand, and he stroked the dog as he spoke.

"Yes, I've asked." Jacki rose and began to roam around the room, feeling her restlessness build. "I'd have a better chance of asking the IRS to forget about my taxes for the next ten years and just send *me* checks." She moved her shoulders up and down in a careless shrug.

Gabriel watched the deep purple sweater she wore as it rose and fell around the swell of her breasts. Abruptly he shifted his gaze back to Malcolm, knowing he had no right to think of Jacki in that light. But he couldn't help himself. Somehow his knack of shutting thoughts out escaped him, when it came to things that concerned Jacki.

"Sooner get blood from a stone," Malcolm agreed. "Don't know how two peas coming from the same pod can be so different."

Sweetheart grumbled, and Gabriel resumed running his hand over the dog's fur. "Some things just don't have an explanation," he commented.

"Tell me about it," Jacki whispered to herself, her eyes on his face.

She saw him studying her curiously and roused herself. She wasn't going to let herself become melancholy. They had a reprieve until a month after Christmas, and that was the main thing.

"Speaking of twins, I wish you were," she told Gabriel, crossing back to him. She began to pick up the

coffee cups that Gabriel had carried into the living room
after dinner. "You do the work of at least two men, but
just right now I could certainly use a couple of hands to
help rebuild the barn." It was always something, wasn't
it? she thought. There didn't seem to be an end to needing things around the ranch.

I need him around the ranch, she thought, looking at
Gabriel. Abruptly she turned and headed for the kitchen,
afraid that he might read her thoughts.

She had just finished getting breakfast ready for the
next morning when Gabriel walked into the kitchen.

He wasn't alone.

With him were two men she had never seen before.
Puzzled, she looked to Gabriel for an explanation. Behind her she heard her grandfather entering the kitchen,
his wheelchair hitting the spot on the threshold that always squeaked.

"Who are your friends?" she asked, wondering if
there was enough for breakfast to stretch out two more
portions. She opened the refrigerator to check on the egg
situation.

"You said last night that you needed a couple more
hands."

With one hand holding the bread sack aloft, she
stopped and stared at Gabriel. He had found two hands
at this hour? She glanced at her wristwatch. It was ten
minutes shy of six o'clock in the morning. Where had the
two men come from? The nearest thunderbolt?

The answer wasn't nearly as funny as she would have
liked it to be. Jacki cleared her throat and set down the
bread. She picked up a spatula. "Their names wouldn't
be Michael and Raphael, would they?" she asked, tak-

ing a firmer grip on the spatula, wishing she had a firmer grip on reality at that moment.

The two men stared at her, and even Gabriel looked mildly surprised. "How did you know?"

"Lucky guess." Her mouth felt dry. It was true. It was really true. He was an angel, and he had brought the gang in to help her. Obviously she came under the heading of those needing a giant miracle.

She wondered what the punishment was for having impure thoughts about an angel.

The shorter, darker of the two men stuck his hand hesitantly in her direction, simultaneously taking off his hat with his other hand. "My name is Rafe, Rafe Sanchez, ma'am."

She shook his hand, still stunned by their appearance, while the other man waited his turn. His hand was firm, strong, callused. He grinned at her, and a gold tooth flashed. Did angels have calluses and gold teeth?

"Mike Mcguire. I'm very pleased to make your acquaintance."

"Likewise." She nodded. A dream. All a dream. It had to be. She turned to look at Gabriel, her eyes huge. "Where did they come from?"

"I called my friend last night. They were staying with him temporarily." Why was she looking so dazed? he wondered. He thought she'd be relieved to get the extra help.

"Of course, your friend," she echoed. God had a telephone and was filling requests.

A giddiness bubbled up inside her, threatening to burst free. She reached behind her for support and accidentally touched the stove. She yelped, bringing the hand to her mouth without thinking.

Gabriel took her hand and guided her to the sink, turning on the cold water. "That could have been nasty," he commented.

Then you'd have to kiss it and make it all better, she thought, but somehow managed to keep the words from coming out.

"You sure can rustle up a crew when you want to," Malcolm said, wheeling himself into the center of the room. Unlike Jacki, he looked very pleased at the turn of events.

Gabriel had expected Jacki to respond similarly. He looked at her now. She offered him a weak smile and turned off the water. She could handle it, she told herself. She could handle it.

Maybe.

"I know it's a little early, but we thought that perhaps you would want to get started clearing away the debris as soon as possible," Rafe suggested. He looked from Jacki to Malcolm, as if confused about whom he would be taking his orders from.

Jacki tried to organize her scattered thoughts and pretend that all this was very normal. "Look, I'm very grateful, but I really can't pay you."

"Breakfast?" Mike asked, raising a brow beneath sandy hair that was badly in need of a cut.

"And a roof overhead. That was what Gabriel told us." Rafe put in.

Maybe it was boring in heaven, playing harps, she thought. Maybe this was slumming for them. Whatever the reason, she'd take what she could get for as long as she could get it. She knew that there would be hell to pay later. Or something along those lines.

"You're keeping the new hands waiting, girl," Malcolm said, pushing himself into the thick of things.

"Knew the minute I laid eyes on you, Gabriel, that our luck was going to change."

"Yes," Jacki said softly. "Me, too."

Numbly she watched as the men sat down.

She couldn't have asked for better workers. But then, they'd had years of practice, she thought. An eternity, no doubt. She shaded her eyes with her hand as she watched Mike and Rafe work on the barn. She had gone into town with Gabriel as soon as the shock of having the two men appear had faded. At the local lumberyard she had managed to arrange for enough credit to obtain the material they needed. After that, everything moved smoothly.

As it had been doing, ever since Gabriel arrived, she thought.

There was little need to tell Rafe and Mike what to do. Self-motivated, they intuitively went about the task of rebuilding the north portion of the barn, as if they were trained carpenters instead of—what? she wondered. Unemployed cowboys? Down-on-their-luck drifters? Bored angels?

Jacki let her hand drop. She didn't have an answer and she no longer cared. Christmas was around the corner. It had always been her favorite time of year, and for now that was all she was going to let herself think about.

At least, that was all she had intended to let herself think about, until the mail came that afternoon. The buoyed feeling she harbored within her as she reached into the mailbox plummeted as soon as she read the first few lines of the neatly typed letter.

She glanced at the bottom, near his signature. He had had his secretary type the letter. He hadn't even had the decency to type his own poison-pen letter.

Damn him!

"Bad news?"

Startled, Jacki whirled around and then told herself that she should have realized he'd be there next to her. Well, he couldn't shield her from this. Heaven could only intervene so far.

"Not bad. Awful." She pushed the letter into her back pocket with a vengeance. To her surprise, Gabriel drew it out again and scanned it. She made no protest. One didn't argue with angels and get very far.

Gabriel folded the letter and frowned. "Is he serious?"

"Caleb is always serious. That was always part of his problem." She walked off and looked at the barn. Rafe and Mike were busy making it whole again. No need, she thought, no need. She'd rather knock it down, knock down the ranch house and everything else in sight. The bank wasn't going to do them in. Caleb was going to beat them to it.

Gabriel stepped up behind her. "He would actually take your grandfather to court and have him declared incompetent?" There was disbelief in his voice. After all, what did angels know about playing dirty, about being greedy?

"He'd be the one to do it. Caleb's a very sharp lawyer, never mind that my grandfather's money made him that way. He wants the money that's in this ranch. A third of it is in his name." She balled her hands into fists, wishing she could drive them into Caleb's soft belly. The membership card he carried to a prestigious health club was for show only. For that—and to make business deals possible, while watching someone else play tennis and sweat. Caleb didn't believe in sweating. Or in being fair

Only in winning. "On the open market the land would bring a good price."

"But you told me he's well-off."

"Never well-off enough. He wants more. He always did." She shook her head in pity as well as in exasperation. "The bank won't get us, but he will." She bit her lip as she turned to look at Gabriel, forgetting her thoughts about him, forgetting everything but the need for someone to lean on, just this one time. "I can't let him do this to Grandpa. The humiliation would kill him."

Gabriel glanced at the envelope's return address before he handed it back to her. The look he gave her was unreadable, yet for some reason she felt comforted. She had no idea why. His next words did nothing to reinforce the feeling.

"Would you mind if I took the day off?"

"No." There was no reason to go on working, anyway. Caleb wanted this resolved now, before he left for his Christmas holiday in the Bahamas. Damn him. She felt tears of anger rising.

Gabriel ran his hand along the back of his neck, thinking. "Could I borrow your Jeep?"

The request surprised her. "I thought you didn't like to drive."

"Not really. But I don't have the time to hitch a ride."

She nodded, without stopping to question his need for the car or ask herself why he didn't just ride his horse. He had said that was what he preferred. It was past the time for questions. She dug into her front pocket and handed him the keys. She didn't even watch as he drove off.

Jacki braced her shoulders, thinking about the straw that broke the camel's back. The letter had been her straw. The last one.

She knew what she was going to do. Go on. She wa
going to go into the house and allow herself to cry for ter
minutes. Then she was going to start decorating for th
holidays, just as she had told her grandfather she would
Christmas was his very favorite time of the year, just a
it was hers. He loved dragging out the old decoration
and telling old stories again and again. And she love
listening to them.

This was going to be their last Christmas at Los Ca
ballos. She was going to see that he enjoyed it. She wasn'
going to let her grandfather know anything was wrong
Maybe tomorrow she would figure a way out of every
thing. Or at least a way to convince her grandfather tha
it would be best to finally let go and sell the ranch.

She'd make him think, she told herself as she took th
first steps up the porch, that it was her idea, that she wa
tired of fighting the odds, tired of fighting the bank. Tha
way there would be no need for Caleb to take action.

She'd die before she'd ever let him know that Cale
wanted to have him declared mentally incompetent, i
Malcolm didn't sell the ranch and give him his share
She'd cut Caleb's heart out before she allowed the trut
to surface.

Jacki felt the letter with her fingers as it stuck out o
her pocket. "Merry Christmas," she muttered to her
self, aware that the words rang hollow.

Chapter Eleven

The silver Christmas tree ball in her hand caught the flickering light from the living room fireplace and scattered it into a multitude of twinkling fragments. The effect was almost hypnotic, Jacki reflected, deep in thought.

He hadn't told her where he was going. And he hadn't come back last night.

Had he left for good?

Now, just before Christmas? She felt sorrow tugging at her heart. Somehow it would have seemed more appropriate for him to go on Christmas Eve, but that was still days away. She had felt that she still had a little time left to spend with him.

Where *was* he?

Feeling nothing, she threaded a hook through the tiny loop on top of the ball, then paused again, aware that her mind was a galaxy away. He had left right after that letter had arrived from Caleb. Had he felt her sense of defeat? Had it transmitted itself to him? Did angels feel defeat, throw in the towel, move on when the odds were stacked? Did they only have an allotted amount of good fortune to spread before disappearing?

So many questions and so few answers. Few? Jacki felt a bitter smile playing across her lips. She had no answers at all.

In the corner Sweetheart dozed at Malcolm's feet, remnants of the popcorn he had been munching scattered around his outstretched paws. Her grandfather was dozing, too. Quite a picture, she thought fondly, fighting back tears.

She sighed, still holding the ball. She thought of Gabriel again. How could he leave them, going as mysteriously as had come? With her Jeep. That part seemed a little odd. What did an angel need with a Jeep? It didn't make sense. But Jacki wasn't sure anymore what made sense and what didn't. She felt overwhelmed. By everything.

Maybe he wasn't an angel. Maybe he was a good con man....

No, she refused to believe that. It was easier to believe that he was an angel.

It suited him.

The tree. Get your mind back on doing this tree, or it'll be Christmas before you hang up the second ornament. With determination she hung up the silver ball and reached for another.

Earlier that morning, to get her mind off Gabriel's absence, she had asked Mike and Rafe to help her bring down the tree from the attic. It stood now, wide, majestic and artificial, in her living room, barren and waiting.

Her grandfather had snorted over the tree when she had first bought it two years ago, but she had managed to make him see the wisdom in it. She hated killing anything, and the thought of cutting down a living tree so that she could keep it in her house for two weeks had always upset her, even as a child. Her grandfather had eventually grudgingly admitted that the tree looked almost real.

But it wasn't. It was artificial. As artificial as her present enthusiasm for decorating it. Christmas had always been a magical time for her, but this year, despite all that Gabriel had done for her, the season was empty because of the threat that hung over her. Because she knew that she would lose him soon.

She glanced at her watch. She had lost track of how many times she had looked at her wrist since early this morning. It was almost five. Gabriel hadn't come home last night, and, until he wasn't sitting opposite her at the dinner table, she hadn't realized how accustomed she had become to having him around. Until she hadn't heard him talking to her grandfather over coffee. Until the sun had risen overhead and he hadn't been there to share it with her, working alongside her. There was no lack of conversation; Mike and Rafe saw to that. Between the two of them there had been words galore. But the words had all seemed hollow to her.

She hadn't realized how empty emptiness was until it had taken over every corner of her soul.

Soul. That was what she was probably risking, if there was such a thing, she thought, trying to be philosophical. One probably forfeited it by trying to seduce an angel. That was what she had practically done in the shack, until that crash of thunder had warned her and brought her back to her senses. Tried to seduce him. She wished she hadn't lost her courage.

You won't know what emptiness is until he's gone for good.

Well, isn't he? she thought. If he wasn't gone for good, then where was he? He had always been as good as his word, and he had said he'd be back last night. And here it was, practically twenty-four hours later, and there was no sign of him.

She felt tears gather in her eyes, tears of sadness, of confusion, of helplessness. She was grateful that her grandfather was asleep and couldn't see her now. She had never felt this dejected, this forlorn in her life. It was an effort to contain a sob as she stood still, her body frozen in malaise, with the second silver ball in her hand.

"You'll never get that tree decorated if you take this long deciding where to place each ball."

She swung around, her heart in her throat. "You're back!"

She wanted to throw her arms around him, to bury her face in his shoulder, to run her hands through his hair and assure herself that it was really him, that he was really here. Only the greatest of control kept her from flinging herself at him.

He slipped out of his jacket and let it rest neatly on the love seat. "I'm sorry, but business took longer than I expected."

She attempted to appear nonchalant and simply shrugged her shoulders in response. She doubted that she'd pulled it off. "It happens, I suppose."

He began to thread hooks through the neatly lined-up silver and red balls that still remained in the first box. "Don't you want to know where I was?"

Yes! Yes, of course I do. "Maybe I'm learning not to ask questions, like you." She saw an amused smile on his lips. He knew her by now.

He handed her a red ball, offering the hook end first. She took it from him tentatively, he noted. "I like you asking questions. I like you just the way you are."

Melting me, he's melting me. Does he have any idea what he's doing to me? And why? Why would he, when we can't—? Or can we—? Was that where he was, finding out if perhaps we could—? She felt consumed by questions too absurd to put into words.

"Okay." She turned to face him, still holding the ball he'd given her. "Where were you?"

He guided her hand to a branch and watched as she hung up the ball, then gave her a nod of approval before answering. "In Newport Beach." He drew a thin envelope from his shirt pocket. "This is addressed to you."

"You picked up my mail?" She took it from him, eyeing it suspiciously. The tree was forgotten.

"In a manner of speaking. Do you mind?"

She glanced up from the unopened envelope. "Do I mind what?" Make something clear. Make just one thing clear to me. I'm wading through swirling mists in the dark, without a guide.

"The tree." He indicated it with his eyes. "Would you mind if I helped you decorate it? It's been ages since I dressed a Christmas tree."

"I'm sure it has," she murmured. "Go right ahead." The envelope bore her name on it and nothing more. The handwriting looked familiar, but she couldn't place it immediately.

As she took out the letter, a white, rectangular piece of paper fluttered out and fell gracefully to her feet. Jacki stooped to pick it up, and then her mouth fell open. It was a check. A check with her brother's signature on it. She looked toward Gabriel, but he appeared utterly engrossed in trimming the tree. He acted as if the fate of the world depended upon his decision about where to hang the next decoration. That would have struck her as unusual, had it not been for the check she held in her hand.

Quickly she scanned the letter. "How—how did you get this?" she asked, her voice scarcely above a whisper. She had almost asked, How did you do this?

He paused and looked at her. He wanted to enjoy her reaction. He loved the way she responded to everything around her, the way her eyes opened wide when she was excited. The effort he had put into arranging this moment was worth it, just to see her.

Then he turned back to the tree. The figure of a little drummer boy came next. He smiled at the boy before he hung him up. "He handed it to me."

"He . . . handed . . . it to you." The words dribbled out of her mouth. Jacki stared at Gabriel, dazed. Caleb never parted with money. It was his cardinal rule. "Before or after you pointed your gun at him?"

"I'm not allowed to carry a gun," Gabriel told her quietly.

"No, of course not. You wouldn't have to," she mumbled, reading the letter a second and then a third time. It told her in an economy of words that was so typical of her brother that he had thought things over, and perhaps it would be to everyone's advantage if she and their grandfather continued running the ranch, rather than selling it. He was enclosing a check for her to pay off the second trust deed her grandfather had taken out. Gabriel had informed him of the sum. She could pay him back whenever she had the money. No interest would be involved.

"No interest," she repeated, looking again at Gabriel. Slowly she refolded the letter and pushed it back into the envelope. "Was he on his deathbed?"

Gabriel reached for a few popcorn kernels from the bowl on the coffee table before he picked up another decoration. "Looked perfectly healthy to me."

She put the palm of her hand to her head, as if the action could help her catch hold of her thoughts and make them clearer. "Wait. What were you doing there in the first place?"

Gabriel circled the tree, taking three decorations with him. His voice came back to her slightly disembodied. Somehow that seemed rather appropriate. "Paying a visit."

She wanted to follow him, but stayed where she was, unable to move. "You know him?"

"I felt as if I did, after all those stories Malcolm told me."

She heard a decoration fall, then his intake of breath as he bent to pick it up. It all sounded so normal. But she knew it wasn't. None of it was. She sighed, letting her shoulders sag in a temporary admission of defeat. "I don't understand."

She jerked when he came up behind her and put his hands on her shoulders. "Jacki." He slowly turned her around to face him. "Did you ever stop to think that some things are enjoyed better when they're not fully explored?"

He was still holding a figure in his hand. Jacki glanced down and saw that it was an angel. How appropriate, she thought with a sting. A miniature.

"Maybe your brother just wanted to do something nice for you for Christmas." He ran his hand along her cheek and felt her tremble slightly beneath his touch. The ache was there within him, full and vibrant. It never left him now, he realized. Soon, he fervently hoped, soon. But not before he told her. "From what I gather it's about time."

She nodded her head. "More like way overdue. If nothing else, he owes this to Grandpa for putting him through college. Of course, he never saw it that way— until now."

Her eyes studied Gabriel's face. The haunting planes and angles, the strength. It was too rugged-looking to belong to an angel. Except for the eyes. The eyes most definitely could.

Since when are you such an expert on what angels are supposed to look like?

Maybe he wasn't an angel.

But he had to be. The check in her pocket proved it. No one on earth could have convinced Caleb to part with money for *this old horse ranch*, as he used to refer to Los Caballos. If she had tried to cling to any doubts before, they were all gone now. This was the final brick in the wall.

"You worked a miracle," she said softly, waiting for him to agree with her. Or to deny it. With her whole heart and soul she wanted him to deny it.

He shrugged, a little uncomfortable at the display of gratitude. "It's the season for them."

He released her. If he didn't, he'd pull her to him and lose himself in her scent, in her softness, making himself believe that things were going to work out.

But he was afraid. For the very first time in his existence he tasted fear. What if he told her and she turned away? Looked at him with fear or disbelief? He didn't want to chance that, not yet. He knew he would have to soon. Things were getting out of hand. But right now he held himself in check. To do anything else wouldn't be fair to her. He owed her the truth, before anything else happened between them.

"Want to finish the tree?"

She nodded, not trusting her voice. For a second she had thought he was going to kiss her, but he hadn't. Angels had great willpower, she thought dryly. She wouldn't know about such things. She was a mere mortal and consumed by desire.

They heard a loud snore slice the air, and when they looked in Malcolm's direction, he was rousing himself, the snore having woken him up, as well as the dog. Sweetheart was on his feet in an instant, claiming his position next to Gabriel.

Malcolm wheeled himself closer to the pair. "Gabriel!" There was no mistaking the pleasure that filled his voice. "We'd just about given you up, boy. Thought maybe a touch of freedom proved to be too tempting." He leaned over to shake Gabriel's hand.

Gabriel laughed. "Working here is freedom, Malcolm."

She loved the way a smile consumed his features, making them soft, making her heart hum. She tried to memorize everything about him, knowing that it would have to last her a long time.

"Glad you feel that way." Malcolm sneaked a look toward his granddaughter and pretended to lower his voice. "You should've seen Jak. She looked as if she was pining away."

Jacki began to deny his observation, but Gabriel's expression stopped her. He does care if I care, she thought. She could see it in his eyes. She forgot to chide her grandfather for his loose tongue.

The smile Gabriel gave her was warm. It reflected the emotions that were brewing within him. So she did care. He had thought he felt it in her kiss, in the way her body moved against his, but had wondered if perhaps he was deluding himself. It had been, after all, a long time since he had held a woman, since he had loved a woman.

Maybe there was a chance she'd understand, after all.

Feeling suddenly elated and hopeful, Jacki moved behind the wheelchair and threaded her arms around her grandfather's neck. "Gabriel was gone on business, Grandpa."

Malcolm automatically patted her arm and turned slightly in his chair, but his eyes remained on Gabriel. "Oh?"

Jacki decided to let him read the letter from Caleb on his own. She released her grandfather and moved before him. In her hand she held the envelope. "For us, so it seems."

Malcolm snatched the envelope from her. "Don't tease your old grandpa."

"Old?" Her eyebrows rose high on her head. "Since when did you get old?" She heard Gabriel laugh behind her. How easily she had come to love everything about him, his laugh, the sound of his voice, even his silence.

Don't leave me, Gabriel, she prayed. Find a way to stay. Please.

"Purely a figure of speech." Malcolm yanked the letter out of the envelope and squinted at the page. Ever so lightly, Jacki slid the glasses that were resting on top of his head back into position on his nose. He looked as if he was going to say something sharp to her about her presumption, but the words in the letter stopped him. His eyes grew round. "Godda—"

"Mmm, Grandpa," Jacki interrupted in a low voice. "I don't think you should say that in front of Gabriel."

"Why?" The shaggy head bobbed up, and he squinted at Gabriel, trying to refocus behind the glasses. Giving up, he snatched them off his face. "He's no saint. He's a man. He's heard a hell of a lot worse. Right, boy?"

Jacki opened and closed her mouth and let the comment pass. She'd confide her suspicions to her grandfather later, when they were alone, when she was sure he wouldn't laugh at her.

Gabriel had gone back to decorating the tree, taking pleasure in his work. He looked over his shoulder before he reached up high for an overhead branch. "In my time," he admitted.

She was tempted to ask him what time that was, B.C. or A.D., but that, too, she let pass. Right now her grandfather was happy, the ranch was saved, the horses were in foal, and for the moment, just for the moment, Gabriel was here, next to her. Many women made do on less. Much less.

Maybe she'd be among them soon, but right now she wasn't, and it was right now that she was going to enjoy.

"Is this some sort of a trick?" Malcolm asked Jacki, waving the check.

Jacki bit her lower lip. "Gabriel says it's not."

"How did you—?" And then Malcolm laughed heartily, slapping the letter across his leg. "Gabriel, you sly devil, you."

"Wrong again, Grandpa," Jacki murmured under her breath as she opened another box of balls.

Malcolm craned his neck in order to see her better. "What?"

"Nothing," she answered hurriedly. "Well, let's finish up this tree before it's Easter. Gabriel, would you bring me the ladder from the attic? We're going to need it to decorate the top branches."

Unless, of course, you intend to fly up and do the honors, she thought. But even that didn't dampen her spirits.

Gabriel nodded and began to leave.

She saw his jacket on the love seat. "Don't forget your jacket," she called after him, then told herself that it was a dumb thing to say. Angels probably didn't feel cold or heat.

But this angel felt. Or acted as if he did. When he kissed her. She could tell the difference between polite indulgence and earnest participation. And Gabriel had most definitely been participating. Even if it was against his will.

He returned to take his jacket and offered her a smile in exchange. "Thanks."

"Wouldn't want you to get sick and miss Christmas." She watched him put on the jacket. The back of his black hair brushed against the collar and touched his shoulders. She wanted to reach out and touch them, too.

He grinned and left.

A thought suddenly struck her. Could he be thrown out of paradise because of what she made him feel? Would this be the way she'd pay him back for all the good he had done? By getting him expelled from heaven?

What did expelled angels do? Did they come back as mortals? Hope grew within her breast, but she pushed it back. She couldn't do that to him.

But what of her? Dear Lord, when he left, what of her? She felt tears suddenly sting her eyes. One fell, and she brushed it aside angrily. Crying would do her no good. Nothing would.

"Tears of happiness, Jak?" Malcolm asked, his voice soft and understanding. He still held the letter in his hand.

She had forgotten he was there. And that he could see her.

"Yes, something like that," she sniffed. She made herself busy on the other side of the tree, willing away the loneliness that was fighting for possession of her soul.

He's back for now, just hold on to that, she told herself. It was all she had.

Chapter Twelve

 W e're going to have ourselves a party, a slam-bang, great big party," Malcolm declared happily when Gabriel returned with the ladder. "I don't know what the hell came over Caleb, but I'm not asking."

Jacki flashed Gabriel a smile as he set up the ladder. Her moment of self-pity had dissipated. In its place were gratitude and relief, overwhelming relief. Now she would never have to tell her grandfather that Caleb had threatened him with public humiliation.

And she owed that to Gabriel. She owed him, she knew, an awful lot. Since he had come, her life had been turned around. The hope she had stored within her all those hard years had bloomed and spread, becoming a garden of thriving flowers, where once there had been nothing but barren desert.

He had, in essence, worked miracle after miracle for her. But he wouldn't be able to accomplish the biggest miracle of all. She was in love with him, and there was nothing on earth she could do about it. Nothing on earth, but maybe in heaven—?

She smiled sadly to herself. She doubted that angels could renounce their wings. Things like that were only possible in fairy tales and movies. Real life didn't work that way.

How real was this situation? she asked herself.

"I want to have the party on Christmas Eve," Malcolm was saying. "We'll invite all our old friends. It's been a long time since this old place has seen a shindig." He glanced at the wheelchair. "Since before I couldn't dance." But even his condition didn't put a damper on his enthusiasm this time. "Time to brighten up these old halls. See to it, Jak, right after you give this to Saunders."

Jacki nodded, hearing only a third of what her grandfather was saying. She tucked the check into her back pocket.

Gabriel studied her expression and wondered why she wasn't happier. There was a smile on her face, but it didn't quite reach her eyes. They were sad. Why? He would have thought she'd be overjoyed. The threat that had been hanging over her head and her grandfather's head since he arrived had been taken away. He had done everything he could think of to make things right for her.

Because he loved her.

He hadn't thought he could, not really anymore, and not so quickly. His emotions had been restrained, almost frozen for so long. But it had taken only the light in her eyes, the quick flash of her smile to prove him wrong, to make him remember what it was like to be alive again. To be a *part* of life again.

But she wasn't happy, and he wondered why.

* * *

Saunders looked impatiently at Jacki and Gabriel the next day as they walked in. He had clearly allowed his secretary to admit them with the greatest of displeasure, appearing certain that the purpose of their visit was to present another plea for an extension.

"Jaclyn, I'm afraid that I have only—" he glanced at the gold clock that stood on his desk "—five minutes to spare, and even that is stretching it."

"This won't take long," she promised. Before he could comment on that, she placed the check she had been holding on his desk.

Saunders barely glanced at it. "What's this?"

"It's a check, Mr. Saunders." She savored every syllable.

"Yes, I see, but—"

"Made out to my grandfather and endorsed over to the bank. I believe that the amount is correct and that everything is in order."

She could tell by the way his eyes widened that although he had given her that extension, Saunders hadn't expected the extra time to amount to anything. The bank was set to foreclose on the ranch at the end of January. She would have bet that the man had marked his calendar for a day that would be convenient to have a public auction. It wasn't that he was particularly hard-hearted, just totally business-oriented. It wasn't something he enjoyed doing, but it was necessary.

But this time Leif Saunders was wrong. He rose from his seat and looked from Jacki to Gabriel, then shifted his eyes back to her face. Jacki saw astonishment in his gaze and noticed that he avoided meeting Gabriel's eyes.

There was something there, she thought. Saunders feels it, too. She tried to dwell on the positive and not let the negative engulf her. Time enough for that later, when

Gabriel was gone. And he would be gone soon. She knew
that, felt it in her heart. All the miracles she needed had
been performed.

Save one.

"You don't know how pleased I am to see this, Jac
lyn," Saunders said in a deep voice, the one everyone
knew he reserved for clients who paid their accounts in
full. Pleasure, as much as he could apparently bring
himself to exhibit, was evident on his face.

"Not nearly half as pleased as I am to give it to you.
This closes our account." She relished the simple words
as she said them.

"Yes, yes, it does." He picked the check up and au
tomatically turned it over to check the endorsement.
Everything was in order. His smile grew, a line splitting
an alabaster plane. The past seemed to have been forgot
ten, as if it had never existed. "Please don't hesitate to
call on us again. The bank is always open to people like
you and your grandfather."

Right. Still, she couldn't fault him completely. He had
only been doing his job—to the letter. Jacki shook the
man's hand and took her leave.

"I'll remember that." She turned and walked out of
the office. "And hope I never have to come here again
except to make a deposit," she whispered to Gabriel with
a grin as they left the bank.

Suddenly she felt like shouting.

She stood outside and took a deep breath. The air was
crisp, cool, a typical winter day for the region. "Free,
Gabriel, we're actually free. God, it feels so wonder
ful."

He linked his fingers with hers, thinking how right her
hand felt in his. As if it belonged. As if he belonged. "I
know exactly what you mean."

Jacki turned to look at him. He'd said it so seriously.
Did being an angel mean confinement to him? Was that
why he had volunteered to come to her aid? She had a
sudden, giddy image of a row of angels, listening to a drill
sergeant head angel rattle off assignments that were being
offered. She ran her hand over her mouth to keep from
laughing aloud. At this moment everything felt wonderful. She savored the freedom, the day, and his hand in
hers.

"Will you stay until the Christmas Eve party?" she
asked suddenly, tightening her fingers on his. As if that
would make him stay, if he had to go, she thought ruefully. But she kept her fingers linked with his.

"Why wouldn't I?"

"No reason." She shrugged casually.

Every reason in the world, or out of it, she thought, a
tinge of sadness throwing a shadow over her moment of
triumph, even now.

Did she think he had to leave? Or did she want him to?
No. He knew her by now. He'd know if she wanted him
to go. But what was the apprehension in her eyes?

He made his mind up to tell her everything on Christmas Eve.

The days seemed to race by. Too soon, she thought,
too soon. It was Christmas Eve before she had time to get
her mind in order. To get her heart in order.

Jacki took great care getting dressed on the night of the
party. Frank Morgan had insisted on sending over his
cook to make all the party preparations. He was a good
man, she thought. Just not the man for her.

And neither was Gabriel. At least Frank was a man.
Gabriel wasn't a man at all. If she had had any doubts
about that, the appearance of Caleb's check had can-
celed them out.

No, she thought, running a brush through her hair an
letting it flow free about her bare shoulders. Gabri
might not be a man, but he was the one she wanted.

She put on a lavender dress that just skimmed h
shoulders and came in at the waist before it flowed fr
just above her knees. Gabriel had never seen her in
dress, she realized, only jeans and shirts. She intended t
make his mouth water—if that was possible.

Jacki studied her reflection in the mirror. Her han
were trembling, she noticed. Stop it. It doesn't make an
difference what you wear. Angels don't care about suc
things.

She wasn't convinced. Something, something had t
work. What, she had no idea.

Her bangs tumbled rebelliously over her forehead. Th
was the best she could do, she thought. She hardly ev
fussed over her hair. Clips and braids had always seeme
like enough before, but not now. With a sigh she tucke
her hair behind her ears.

Jacki clipped on big hoop earrings. She watched the
gleam in the light. They'd been her mother's. That helpe
a little, she decided. She slipped backless, high-heele
sandals onto her feet, took a breath and made her wa
out to join the party.

Noise and laughter met her like a wave as soon as sl
opened her bedroom door. She scarcely heard tl
sounds. She only knew she wanted to find Gabriel, to l
with him for however long she had left.

Gabriel stood at the far side of the room. He saw h
as soon as she entered the living room, despite the nun
ber of bodies between them. He would have noticed h
if she had been wearing sackcloth and ashes. But sl
wasn't. The simple dress accented every inch of h
womanliness and made him aware again just how muc
he ached for her. Her face was almost exotic tonight. Th

nocent look he had found so appealing now blended
with the air of a beautiful woman who knew what and
whom she wanted.

Would he be the one, after he'd told her everything?

Jacki saw him. She could feel him looking at her. Did
e like what he saw? Ammunition. She wished desper-
tely for an argument, something substantial to tip the
cales in her favor.

She had absolutely no idea what it took to make an
ngel love her.

Before she could make her way toward him, she was
aught up in the party, as people she had known most of
er life expressed their congratulations or wished her a
1erry Christmas.

Jacki looked toward Gabriel. There was only one thing
1e wanted to make her Christmas truly merry.

The party went on for hours. It was hard not to get
aught up in the festivities. It was such a joyous occa-
on. The fact that it was Christmas Eve merely com-
ounded their celebration. But finally she managed to
ip away. She discovered that she needed air and a little
eace and quiet to gather her thoughts.

He'd be gone soon.

One more miracle, she thought, staring at the star-
udded sky. The sky had looked just like this the night
e first arrived. Oh, please, I know I've gotten so much,
ut please, please, just one more miracle. I need him
1ore than You do. She folded her hands before her in
1pplication.

Terrific. Now you're bargaining with God for perma-
ent possession of an angel. She shook her head, despair
eginning to seep in.

"What are you doing out here?"

She turned, startled. He slipped a shawl over he shoulders. Considerate to the end, she thought sadl Was this the end? Oh, God, she hoped not. "Trying t get my thoughts together."

He had stood watching her a moment before speal ing. She looked so lovely, he'd hated to disturb her. B he had made himself a promise, and Christmas Eve wa almost over.

He felt the strong pull between them. Being out her with her made him ache for her, ache to hold her, to lov her, to have her gaze at him with that cloudy look of de sire he had seen come into her eyes in the shack.

He ran his knuckles along her cheek. "What are yo thinking about so hard?"

"You," she said in a whisper that feathered along h face.

"Is that why you look so sad?" He moved to kiss he to cover her lips with his own and lose himself in th sweetness he knew was there. Just one more time befo the truth was out.

Jacki moved back. Please, please don't torture me th way, she begged silently. "Yes."

He looked at her for a long moment. It was comin He knew it was coming. But even so, he had to face it. H had promised himself that already. He never went bac on his word, not even to himself.

"Jacki, what's wrong?"

She looked down, feeling lost, hopeless. "I can't go o like this—"

He took a deep breath. "Then you know?"

"Yes," she cried, aware that tears were filling her eye He was going to admit it to her, admit it and then vanis from her life. The ache that materialized in her brea threatened to overwhelm her.

Then it did matter to her. He fought off his disappointment. But it was no use. He felt devastated. "How did you find out?"

"How did I—?" Her voice trailed away as she looked at him. "It was so obvious." She laughed sadly. "Every time I turned around, there was another arrow pointing to it. Every time I tried to talk myself out of it, you did something to prove me wrong. I tried not to believe it, but I couldn't hide from it any longer."

She had lost him, utterly and completely lost him. He hadn't the vaguest idea what she was talking about anymore. He was almost certain that they couldn't be talking about the same thing. Perhaps they never had been.

"Jacki—" he took hold of her arms "—what are you talking about?"

"That you're an angel, of course," she fairly shouted at him. Why was he toying with her this way? Did it give him pleasure? No. Angels weren't like that. At least, not her angel.

For a moment there was nothing but silence between them. In the background the sounds of the party were still going on, but out here there were only night sounds and silence. The drumming of her blood grew too loud in her ears.

When he finally recovered, he could only whisper one word. "What?"

"You heard me." Jacki's voice sounded hoarse, even to her. The ache in her throat increased. She was going to cry, and she didn't want to. She turned her head away from him to hide the tears that were coming. "I know your secret. You're an angel."

"You're serious." It wasn't a question so much as an astonished conclusion.

She shook her head numbly.

And then, to her everlasting surprise, Gabriel began t
laugh, laugh so hard that he couldn't speak for sever
long moments. Speechless, he hugged her to himself, an
she felt his laughter against her.

"What are you laughing at?" she demanded. Wasn
it enough that he had stripped her of her defenses, whe
there was no chance for happiness? Did he have to laug
at her, as well?

"Oh, God." Gabriel gulped in air as he wiped away th
tears that had come to his eyes as he laughed. "I've bee
called a lot of things in my time, Jacki, but never a
angel. Where—?" He laughed again, his hands on he
shoulder to steady himself. "Where did you get tha
idea?"

She looked at him uncertainly. "Well," she began, nc
allowing herself to hope. Maybe he wasn't allowed t
share his identity, after all. "To begin with, there's you
name."

"Gabriel was my mother's fancy. The Goodfellow wa
my father's contribution."

"Goodfellow's rather an odd last name."

"Not if you're an Indian. Have you ever heard of Na
vajos, Jacki?" His grin was soft, easy. She was ado
able, and he didn't think he could love her more than I
did at this moment.

"Of course I've heard of Navajos," she retorted, the
stopped. "You're a Navajo?"

"Just half."

She paused, thinking. It helped explain a lot c
things—if it was true. Fear of disappointment kept h
suspicious. "Is that why you seemed to charm Swee
heart and the horses?"

He nodded. It was something he took for grante
"I've always had a natural affinity with animals. Mc

Navajos do. We also don't believe it's polite to compete," he reminded her.

Yes, she remembered hearing that somewhere once. Jacki let that go for the moment. "All right, why can't you vote?"

There was a long silence. "I'm not allowed to." He turned to look into her eyes, seeking the understanding he now knew was there. This was the secret he had prepared himself to share with her. "Ex-convicts can't."

"You're an ex-convict?" she echoed.

There was only surprise in her voice, but not the loathing, not the contempt he had feared. She wasn't going to distance herself from him. Maybe she would understand, after all.

Besides, it was time she knew. He put his hands on the porch railing, looking not at her but at the sky, looking for strength. He had never been one to explain himself to anyone. He needed to explain himself now, to her.

"My younger brother got in with the wrong crowd a few years ago. You know the kind. They felt the world owed them something, because of the life they had had to put up with." The slightest bitterness outlined his smile, but then it was gone. "It might be the nineteen-nineties, but life on a reservation hasn't progressed all that much from a hundred years ago. There's a lot of pain there, a loss of self-esteem."

But not for you, she thought. There might have been pain, but never a loss of self-esteem. Suddenly she was aware that she'd believed him for the moment.

"Lucas was with them when they held up a liquor store. Guns were involved, although luckily no one was hurt. I knew that Lucas would never be able to survive prison if he was caught, and the trap was tightening."

He shrugged, feigning indifference, but she saw through it.

"He was set up to take the fall. A little like Caleb had been by his so-called friends," he said, looking at her. "I took the blame for him. Three years in prison, time off for good behavior. It was a small price to pay in the end. Lucas's gone on to college. He's going to make something of himself. The debt's been paid."

She could see him doing that, giving up a piece of himself so that someone else could be saved.

"And ex-convicts can't vote." He leaned one hip against the railing. The lights from the house spilled onto the porch, but he saw only her. "That's what I meant when I said I had taken part in the system. The justice system." He smiled as he looked at her. She wasn't totally satisfied, he realized. "Next?"

"How about those ranch hands that came out of the blue? Michael and Rafael?" The names of two other angels, she thought, but kept the thought to herself.

He laughed as she pointedly said their names. "Just some people I knew, who had fallen on hard times. When your belly's empty, you'll work hard to fill it. And they needed to work to keep their own self-esteem up. They didn't want to go on staying with my friend and living on charity. I told them that once things got better, you'd be able to pay them in cash."

"And the loan extension?" she insisted. "Saunders wouldn't extend a loan for his own mother."

"He would, if it was pointed out to him that it was just before Christmas, and that it could generate a lot of ill will in the community to have someone of Malcolm's standing thrown off his ranch."

"You said that to Saunders?"

"In so many words."

She clapped her hands and laughed. She would have loved to have seen Saunders's face when he wrestled with that one. But there was even a knottier skein for Gabrie to untangle. "But how did you get Caleb to change his mind about selling the ranch? And how did you get him to send money? Anything short of an angel would have been thrown out of his office for that kind of a suggestion."

"He was about to have me thrown out," he admitted easily. "But Malcolm had told me enough about Caleb, so that I could mention to him that perhaps his landholding partners might be interested in his run-in with the law—"

"Blackmail," she breathed.

"In a manner of speaking. Disapprove?"

"What do you think?" She knew her eyes shone. "Poor Caleb. He must have wanted to spit bullets." Then she sobered. "But what about all those things that happened every time we kissed? The power failure, the earthquake and the thunder?"

She certainly had built up a case in her mind, he thought fondly. "Just simple coincidences, Jacki, nothing more." He touched her face softly. He had told her the truth, and she hadn't turned from him. That was miracle enough for him. "Convinced of my mortality yet?"

"Almost." She put a hand on his shoulder and looked into his eyes. "Who was the 'Boss' you were talking to that night I came with the extra blanket?" It seemed almost silly now, and yet she had to get this one last thing cleared up.

"What?" He was sure he hadn't heard her correctly.

Feeling slightly foolish, she rushed ahead, anyway. As she spoke with animation, her shawl slipped from her shoulders. "I found you in the corral, and you were discussing the ranch's problems with 'Boss.'"

Carefully he rearranged the shawl on her shoulders. He kept the laughter out of his eyes. "Don't you talk to your horse?"

"Your horse?" she echoed, nearly choking.

"Who did you think I was talking to?"

She looked at the floor. "God."

He crooked a finger under her chin and lifted it. "If I were, it'd be to thank him for bringing you into my life."

"All right. One last thing." This had been the start of it all. "What were you doing in the chapel that day?"

"Same as you. Praying for a miracle." He gathered her into his arms. "As far as I'm concerned, I found it. You're my miracle, Jacki." His expression grew somber as he went on. "You're my beginning, my truth, my destiny. I knew that the minute I saw you. I've been to hell and back in my time, and I want my piece of heaven for it now. But I don't want to be an angel, because as far as I know, angels aren't allowed to have the kind of thoughts I'm having about you."

She grinned, relieved. "What are you going to do about them?"

"Well, your grandfather's already offered me money if I take you off his hands."

She loved the feel of his arms around her, and reveled in the warmth it created through her. "He did, huh?"

He could tell by the look on her face that the idea was acceptable. "Yes. Will you marry me, Jacki? Will you let me stay on here and go on helping you with the ranch?"

"Just try and get away."

Before he bent to kiss her, Gabriel cocked a brow and looked toward the sky. "Thanks, Boss," he murmured under his breath.

Jacki jumped back, staring at him.

He grinned. "Just keeping you on your toes. After all, a little mystery in a marriage will always keep it fresh."

And I intend to keep this marriage fresh for a long, long time.''

"You're on.''

As she lost herself in his kiss, Jacki knew that he would always be her special angel, wings or no wings.

* * * * *

Take 4 bestselling love stories FREE

Plus get a FREE surprise gift!

PASSPORT TO ROMANCE
SWEEPSTAKES RULES

1. **HOW TO ENTER:** To enter, you must be the age of majority and complete the official entry form, or print your name, address, telephone number and age on a plain piece of paper and mail to: Passport to Romance, P.O. Box 9056, Buffalo, NY 14269-9056. No mechanically reproduced entries accepted.

2. All entries must be received by the CONTEST CLOSING DATE, DECEMBER 31, 1990 TO BE ELIGIBLE.

3. **THE PRIZES:** There will be ten (10) Grand Prizes awarded, each consisting of a choice of a trip for two people from the following list:
   i) London, England (approximate retail value $5,050 U.S.)
   ii) England, Wales and Scotland (approximate retail value $6,400 U.S.)
   iii) Carribean Cruise (approximate retail value $7,300 U.S.)
   iv) Hawaii (approximate retail value $9,550 U.S.)
   v) Greek Island Cruise in the Mediterranean (approximate retail value $12,250 U.S.)
   vi) France (approximate retail value $7,300 U.S.)

4. Any winner may choose to receive any trip or a cash alternative prize of $5,000.00 U.S. in lieu of the trip.

5. **GENERAL RULES:** Odds of winning depend on number of entries received.

6. A random draw will be made by Nielsen Promotion Services, an independent judging organization, on January 29, 1991, in Buffalo, NY, at 11:30 a.m. from all eligible entries received on or before the Contest Closing Date.

7. Any Canadian entrants who are selected must correctly answer a time-limited, mathematical skill-testing question in order to win.

8. Full contest rules may be obtained by sending a stamped, self-addressed envelope to: "Passport to Romance Rules Request", P.O. Box 9998, Saint John, New Brunswick, Canada E2L 4N4.

9. Quebec residents may submit any litigation respecting the conduct and awarding of a prize in this contest to the Régie des loteries et courses du Québec.

10. Payment of taxes other than air and hotel taxes is the sole responsibility of the winner.

11. Void where prohibited by law.

COUPON BOOKLET OFFER TERMS

To receive your Free travel-savings coupon booklets, complete the mail-in Offer Certificate on the preceeding page, including the necessary number of proofs-of-purchase, and mail to: Passport to Romance, P.O. Box 9057, Buffalo, NY 14269-9057 The coupon booklets include savings on travel-related products such as car rentals, hotels, cruises, flowers and restaurants. Some restrictions apply. The offer is available in the United States and Canada. Requests must be postmarked by January 25, 1991. Only proofs-of-purchase from specially marked "Passport to Romance" Harlequin® or Silhouette® books will be accepted. The offer certificate must accompany your request and may not be reproduced in any manner. Offer void where prohibited or restricted by law. LIMIT FOUR COUPON BOOKLETS PER NAME, FAMILY, GROUP, ORGANIZATION OR ADDRESS. Please allow up to 8 weeks after receipt of order for shipment. Enter quickly as quantities are limited. Unfulfilled mail-in offer requests will receive free Harlequin® or Silhouette® books (not previously available in retail stores), in quantities equal to the number of proofs-of-purchase required for Levels One to Four, as applicable.

PR-SWPS

OFFICIAL SWEEPSTAKES
ENTRY FORM

Complete and return this Entry Form immediately—the more Entry Forms you submit, the better your chances of winning!
- Entry Forms must be received by **December 31, 1990**
- A random draw will take place on **January 29, 1991**   3-SR-1-SW
- Trip must be taken by **December 31, 1991**

YES, I want to win a PASSPORT TO ROMANCE vacation for two! I understand the prize includes round-trip air fare, accommodation and a daily spending allowance.

Name_____

Address_____

City_____ State_____ Zip_____

Telephone Number_____ Age_____

Return entries to: **PASSPORT TO ROMANCE**, P.O. Box 9056, Buffalo, NY 14269-9056

COUPON BOOKLET/OFFER CERTIFICATE

Item	LEVEL ONE Booklet 1	LEVEL TWO Booklet 1 & 2	LEVEL THREE Booklet 1, 2 & 3	LEVEL FOUR Booklet 1, 2, 3 & 4
Booklet 1 = $100+	$100+	$100+	$100+	$100+
Booklet 2 = $200+		$200+	$200+	$200+
Booklet 3 = $300+			$300+	$300+
Booklet 4 = $400+	____	____	____	$400+
Approximate Total Value of Savings	$100+	$300+	$600+	$1,000+
# of Proofs of Purchase Required	4	6	12	18
Check One	____	____	____	____

Name_____

Address_____

City_____ State_____ Zip_____

Return Offer Certificates to: **PASSPORT TO ROMANCE**, P O Box 9057 Buffalo, NY 14269-9057

Requests must be postmarked by **January 25, 1991**

✂ --

ONE PROOF OF PURCHASE   3-SR-1

To collect your free coupon booklet you must include the necessary number of proofs-of-purchase with a properly completed Offer Certificate

See previous page for details.